Clayton
"Are you afraid of me?"

Lucy trembled involuntarily as his low, sexy drawl skittered up her spine. She tried to ignore the sensation, meeting his gaze with what she hoped was a withering glare.

"In your dreams," she retorted.

"Oh, you'll be there," Clayton replied easily. "I'm going to be seeing a lot of you, Lucy Warner." He reached out and, soft as a whisper, stroked her cheek, mesmerized by the silkiness he met and by the way she became immobile with...

What was that in her eyes? Panic?

Clayton backed away, realizing he'd have to go very slowly with this particular woman.

"It won't matter if you hide behind your kids and try to avoid me," he said gently. "I plan to get close to you, and we're going to be good together—that's a promise."

He grinned his sexy grin. "And a McKinley always keeps his promises."

Dear Reader,

Get Caught Reading. It sounds slightly scandalous, romantic and definitely exciting! I love to get lost in a book, and this month we're joining the campaign to encourage reading everywhere. Share your favorite books with your partner, your child, your friends. And be sure to get caught reading yourself!

The popular ROYALLY WED series continues with Valerie Parv's *Code Name: Prince*. King Michael is still missing—but there's a plan to rescue him! In *Quinn's Complete Seduction* Sandra Steffen returns to BACHELOR GULCH, where Crystal finally finds what she's been searching for—and more....

Chance's Joy launches Patricia Thayer's exciting new miniseries, THE TEXAS BROTHERHOOD. In the first story, Chance Randell wants to buy his lovely neighbor's land, but hadn't bargained for a wife and baby! In *McKinley's Miracle*, talented Mary Kate Holder debuts with the story of a rugged Australian rancher who meets his match.

Susan Meier is sure to please with *Marrying Money*, in which a small-town beautician makes a rich man rethink his reasons for refusing love. And Myrna Mackenzie gives us *The Billionaire Is Back*, in which a wealthy playboy fights a strong attraction to his pregnant, single cook!

Come back next month for the triumphant conclusion to ROYALLY WED and more wonderful stories by Patricia Thayer and Myrna Mackenzie. Silhouette Romance always gives you stories that will touch your emotions and carry you away....

Be sure to *Get Caught Reading!*

Mary-Theresa Hussey

Mary-Theresa Hussey
Senior Editor

Please address questions and book requests to:
Silhouette Reader Service
U.S.: 3010 Walden Ave., P.O. Box 1325, Buffalo, NY 14269
Canadian: P.O. Box 609, Fort Erie, Ont. L2A 5X3

McKinley's Miracle

MARY KATE HOLDER

SILHOUETTE *Romance*®

Published by Silhouette Books

America's Publisher of Contemporary Romance

To my parents, Henry and Mary Holder, who taught me
that anything is possible and whose love and support
lifted me high enough to touch my dream.

 SILHOUETTE BOOKS

ISBN 0-373-19521-4

MCKINLEY'S MIRACLE

Copyright © 2001 by Mary Kathleen Holder

This edition published by arrangement with Harlequin Books S.A.

Visit Silhouette at www.eHarlequin.com

Printed in U.S.A.

MARY KATE HOLDER

has lived all her life in Cowra, central eastern New South Wales. Though romance writing takes up a lot of her time, she also finds pleasure in cross-stitch, cooking, drawing and finding homes for stray animals. She resides with two dogs and two cats, who all guard their own part of the house diligently and would probably complain about her love of country music played often and loud...if they could speak. Though she enjoys the peace and quiet of country life, this hasn't cured her of the travel bug, and she hopes to be setting off very soon to travel overseas.

Dear Reader,

I have always loved words, their power, their splendor, the depths of emotion they can stir. But when I received the call from Silhouette telling me they wanted to buy my novel, I could not find words to describe how it felt. How does one describe a dream come true? Eight years ago I sat down to write a romance novel and began a long journey filled with many lessons. Along the way I had the support of my parents, family, friends and authors I loved to read who were never too busy to write back to me with words of encouragement and advice. I hope you enjoy reading about Clayton and Lucy. Writing their story was a joy for me, and being able to share it with you is a wonderful feeling. To me happy endings are like dreams. They become impossible only when we stop reaching for them.

Best wishes,

Mary Kate Holder

Chapter One

Clayton McKinley was about to order his second beer when the door to the Roadhouse opened and she walked in. He hadn't seen her around before, but in Cable Creek, Australia, there were no strangers, just people you hadn't met. She made her way slowly through the crowd. She was dressed to blend in. Tennis shoes. Blue jeans. Grey sweatshirt. Hair pulled into a ponytail. But the shoes were worn and old. The jeans were faded and snug, drawing his attention to her slim hips and shapely curves. The sweatshirt skimmed high, rounded breasts, the sleeves pushed almost to her elbows. The clip holding her chestnut hair in place was plain gold. She stopped suddenly, her hands drawn into fists at her sides. Seconds later she moved with lightning speed toward the bar. He watched, every muscle in his body tense and alert, a second beer forgotten as she squared her shoulders and walked right up to the meanest man in town.

"Gerry Anderson?"

Around them everything stopped, a testament to the

anger in her voice and the unabashed curiosity of the Saturday-night patrons. Someone pulled the plug on the jukebox. Conversations fell to whispers and then ceased altogether. Every eye in the place was on the slender five-foot-three woman and the burly six-foot man she faced. Gerry turned around, dismissing her with a smirk. Clayton counted that as his first mistake.

"You got the name right, sweetie. What can I do for you?"

She stepped closer to her colossal opponent not even sparing a glance for the two men flanking him. "This is about what I will do to you the next time you bully one of my children."

Gerry laughed. "Your kids? I heard they were strays nobody else wanted." He shook his head. "You should go back where you came from. We don't want your kind here."

She pinned him with a look that could have laid ice on the Simpson Desert in the middle of summer. "They are under my care, Mr. Anderson. That makes them my children. Max is just thirteen years old and thanks to you he spent the last two hours in the emergency ward."

For the first time since she'd spoken his name, Gerry looked uncomfortable. "I don't know what you're talkin' about."

"You deliberately drove your car onto the shoulder of the road, kicking up the loose gravel. It frightened the boy's horse so badly he was thrown."

Her words sparked a simmering anger in Clayton. Gerry had a mile-wide mean streak, but picking on a child was a low act. He thought of his niece, at home safe in her bed. If it had been Molly on that horse Gerry would be the one in the emergency room.

Gerry smiled. "You got no proof it was me."

"I don't know of anyone else in this town with the license plate STUD or the arrogance that goes along with it."

He turned back toward the bar. Clayton counted that as his second mistake. "Damn kid's lyin' through his teeth. I wasn't even there."

"You're a coward."

Her words dropped into the silence with the impact of an unexploded bomb. Gerry turned back to her, pure venom in his eyes. Clayton pushed slowly to his feet.

"Don't start nothin' you can't finish, missy."

"My name is Lucy Warner, not missy."

Clayton did a double take. This was his new neighbour? His first thought was that she looked at least ten years younger than the twenty-five he knew her to be. His second thought was that he wanted to get to know her…a lot better.

"And calling that boy a liar makes you a coward. If I'd been there *you* would have been going to the hospital on life support."

Someone chuckled. Another brave soul clapped. Most however seemed content to watch the showdown with undisguised interest. Gerry glanced at his mates and laughed, but Clayton watched his fist close in rage. Raising a hand to her would be Gerry's last mistake of the night. Clayton would make damn sure of it.

"Some kid can't handle himself on a horse and you blame me? Just go back to the city where you belong and take those delinquents with you."

Lucy seemed unimpressed. "Why? Because if I don't you'll bully me too?"

Gerry shrugged. "All kinds of things can happen to a woman out here."

"You might think you're a tough guy in this town,

Mr. Anderson, and maybe picking on children is what it takes to make you feel like a man," she taunted, raising herself to her full height, squaring her shoulders, her chin high. "But the next time you see one of my children minding their own business you'd better do the same."

When she turned, the crowd parted like the Red Sea before her. Someone whistled encouragement as she walked to the door. On the threshold she looked back and glared at him. "This is the only warning you get, Mr. Anderson. Leave us alone."

Lucy had been this angry at least once in her life before tonight. Right now she couldn't remember it though. Blind fury had pushed her into the pub. Pure adrenaline had fueled her words and dignity had enabled her to walk out.

She didn't remember getting in her car or turning onto the road, leaving the brightly lit hotel car park behind. Now in the darkness, her adrenaline level dropped and Lucy began to tremble. Never in her life had she raised a hand to anyone, man or woman, but Gerry had tempted her. The smug look on his face. The arrogance in his eyes. The crack he'd made about the children being strays. Physically she would have been out of her depth with him. Words had been her only weapon.

According to Gray Harrison, most people here were good, honest folk. They believed in hard work and simple living and had community spirit, that small-town sense of rallying together to help each other in times of crisis. She deferred to Gray's judgement on that. He'd grown up here after all.

The first time Lucy had set eyes on the farmhouse she had known this was where the dream was meant to take shape. At times it still seemed impossible to her that the journey she had started for Megan had brought her this far. It had started out as a promise, the only way Lucy could think to make up to her sister all she had denied Megan in one moment of recklessness.

Being a foster mother and having a degree in social welfare had given her credibility to get the project off the ground. Gray's friendship and the sponsorship of his corporation had sealed it for her. Now it was a reality. A place for troubled teens to find a life away from the streets. Streets that sucked their young lives away. Her own years of experience dealing with troubled street kids had shown her a side to life no child should ever know. The idea for the farm had been her sister's long-cherished dream and now it was within reach. Lucy wasn't about to let Gerry Anderson or anyone like him stand in her way.

Though she was only recognized as foster mother to Katie and Max, the powers that be had allowed her guardianship of the two older kids also. To the bureaucrats this was an experiment and Lucy had to succeed so more kids could be given the chance to come here.

She was so lost in thought that when the car began to jerk, her hands tightened on the steering wheel. When it began to sputter, Lucy pulled off the road, and before she could turn off the engine the car died. She reached across into the glove box and found the small torch she'd tucked in there for emergencies. Alone on a dark, lonely stretch of highway, Lucy looked at the fuel gauge and uttered a curse into the night.

Clayton left the roadhouse twenty minutes after Lucy and had driven barely a mile when he spotted the vehicle off to the shoulder of the road, its hazard lights blinking in the darkness. He dimmed his lights and slowed, pulling in behind. Before he turned off his engine, the driver's door opened and the occupant rushed up to his car. Lucy Warner stood there in the cold wind of an August night. Clayton opened his door and got out. "You really shouldn't approach a strange vehicle on a lonely road."

Lucy didn't hear censure in his voice, just old-fashioned concern. In the glare of his headlights she could make out his strong build. The hat he wore, an Aussie akubra, shadowed his face and her curiosity slipped up a notch.

"It was either stop someone or spend the night here," she said. "I prefer a bed to the back seat of a car. When you pulled up, I figured I'd take my chances."

Clayton pushed his hat back just slightly. He preferred a bed to the back seat as well but he didn't think they knew each other well enough for that discussion. "And if I were someone planning to do you harm?"

Lucy stiffened her backbone and lifted her chin. The thought hadn't occurred to her...but it did now. Gerry hadn't been alone at the pub. What if this man was one of his cronies?

"Then the self-defence classes I took a few years back would be put to the test." He was a big man, broad across the shoulders and at least six feet tall. All the defensive positions in the world would not have saved her if he'd intended to do her harm. She thought she heard him chuckle as he walked to her car.

"What seems to be the problem, Miss Warner?"

Fear slid its icy fingers down her spine. "How do you know my name?"

"You kind of introduced yourself back at the Roadhouse. I'm Clayton McKinley, your neighbour at Cable Downs.''

She crossed her arms beneath her breasts. "Any relation to the local vet?"

"He's my big brother," he replied, pride accompanying the words. "One of them anyway."

Lucy had met Joshua McKinley a week after her arrival. He'd seemed a reserved man with kind eyes. Instinct told her *reserved* was not a word that would apply to his younger brother.

"Thanks for stopping."

"It's my pleasure."

Lucy didn't imagine the slight coaxing tone his baritone voice had taken on with those three words. This man's pleasures weren't something she wanted to poke her nose into. "You don't happen to be a friend of Gerry Anderson do you?"

"I'd rather have no friends if Gerry was the alternative. Loudmouthed bullies with more brawn than brain deserve everything they eventually get."

"Then there must be a huge fall somewhere in his future."

"I'd bet on it." He looked toward the vehicle. "So what's wrong with your car?"

"Everything, according to the mechanic who serviced it last," she said, glancing at the car. "He said if it were a horse he'd have it shot. For now I'm merely out of petrol and wondering if it can get any colder."

"Oh sure it can," he said easily. "There's nothing like an Australian winter to test your mettle. Get in my truck and put the heater on. You'll be warm in no time."

The offer was tempting...far too tempting. "That won't be necessary. If you have a mobile phone I can call the garage and get Rick to bring some fuel out."

Clayton smiled to himself. He couldn't really blame her for being so careful. He'd just warned her about strangers after all. Still, her reply sounded more prickly than cautious. He'd known prickly women before—hell, he'd known all kinds of women before. Every day since he'd hit puberty women had fascinated him. The fact that he would never understand any woman if he lived to be a hundred only intrigued him more.

"Sorry, no mobile phone."

Lucy couldn't hide her surprise. "Everyone and his dog has a mobile telephone these days."

Clayton grinned and stuffed his hands in his coat pockets. "Well, my dog and I do just fine without one," he told her. "And where's yours?"

"At home," she said, wishing she'd never even asked him about the damn phone. Walking to the garage would have been less frustrating. Usually she didn't go anywhere without the mobile, but she hadn't exactly been thinking clearly when she'd stormed out of the house an hour ago. She'd kept her calm while at the emergency room, but once Max was home safe she'd needed to blow off steam.

"I've got a can of fuel in the back of the truck. I'll put it in your car and follow you to the truck stop. That saves you getting a ride back out here."

Lucy liked doing things for herself. But she wanted to get home to Max, and Clayton was offering a solution to her problem.

"Thanks. I'll pay you for the fuel when we get to the station and I get change."

"Forget it."

"I don't like accepting charity."

"Lady, it's a couple of dollars' worth of fuel. Out here that isn't charity. It's simply being neighbourly."

"I still intend to pay you."

Clayton shrugged. "You can try."

Lucy hugged herself against the chill and glanced up to see him shrugging out of the coat he wore. He held the garment out to her. "Put this on." She made no move to take it. "Either put it on or get in the truck."

"And when you freeze to a solid block of ice, what am I supposed to do with you?"

Clayton liked her irritation. He might have to take the long way around to get past her defences but he had a keen sense of direction. "I don't think I'm in any danger, but if it happens you take me back to your place, thaw me out and be gentle about it. What we do after that is up to you, since I'll be at your mercy."

She scowled. "This is serious. Think hypothermia. Frostbite. Pneumonia!"

"If I promise not to die, will you put the coat on?" She hesitated. "Listen, you've got kids waiting at home. The sooner you put this on, the sooner I can fuel up your car and we can get moving."

Lucy couldn't decide what she hated more—the fact that he'd made a very valid point or the confident tone of his voice. She took the coat from him. Nothing she said would make an ounce of difference and she did want to get home. She shrugged into the lambswool coat, its fleecy lining warm from his body heat. It hung to her knees, but right now keeping warm took precedence over style.

Clayton walked to the back of his vehicle. Retrieving the fuel can and a plastic funnel, he came back around to where she stood. In the beam of his headlights he bent down to the task at hand.

"The boy Gerry hurt, will he be all right?"

The question didn't surprise Lucy. The genuine concern that accompanied it did. "He'll be stiff and sore for a few days."

"Joshua said you've got four kids living out here with you."

"Well, Thomas doesn't like to be called a kid but yes."

Clayton let the fuel can drain to the last drop then put the lid on it and capped the petrol tank. He closed the latch and pushed to his feet. "Don't let Gerry get to you."

Lucy buried her hands in the pockets of his coat. "We've done nothing to him."

"Your problem is that he made a bid on the house you're living in. He wasn't overjoyed when Gray decided to rent it out."

"That place was meant for a family. Gerry hardly strikes me as the home-and-hearth type. What woman would have him?"

"None around here, but your place has some of the best grazing land and it borders Anderson Farms at the southernmost boundary where the creek runs through it."

"No wonder he wants me gone."

"There is an upside to this."

"And that would be?"

"We're not all like Gerry. His kind are a very small minority around here."

"You know him pretty well I take it?"

"He's lived here all his life. He likes to drink, pick fights and big note himself, not always in that order. He even did it at school."

"Well, he'll find himself in the hospital if he doesn't heed my warning and leave us alone."

Clayton understood her protective nature. "Just watch

your back. I doubt Gerry's ever had a woman stand up to him...and in public.''

Lucy had known men like him before who bullied those weaker than themselves. ''Thanks for the warning.''

''See if the car starts.'' He stashed the funnel and empty can back in his truck, and by the time he reached her door the engine was idling. ''You take off. I'll be right behind you.''

Clayton walked back to his vehicle before she could offer the protest he anticipated and waited for her to pull onto the road before he started his truck and followed. He'd been busy on the farm this past month and hadn't found time to socialize, but he recalled Josh saying he'd had a call out to the Harrison farm. His brother had forgotten to mention just how pretty the new tenant was. And she had courage...either that or she'd let her anger get the better of her a while ago and hadn't stopped to think about what she was doing. He thought of how protective he and his brothers were of Molly. If Gerry had considered Lucy as an easy target, one he could intimidate into leaving, he'd just gotten a wake-up call.

When word had spread around town that Alma Harrison's rambling, two-story house had been snapped up, the fear of big development was rife. Lucy Warner arrived a few weeks ago and replaced that fear of change with a fear of the unknown. In less than a day it seemed everyone far and wide knew of her plans to make it a home for kids who needed a new start, children who had nowhere else to go.

Clayton and his brothers had backed the idea from the beginning, and though a portion of the townsfolk had initially shied away from what they didn't understand, most people now took the view of live and let live. Except for Gerry.

When Lucy indicated, Clayton slowed his vehicle and followed her into the well-lit service station.

Lucy pulled up beside the petrol pump and cut the engine. She got out and handed the keys to the attendant with a polite "Fill her up." Walking back to where Clayton had parked, she stopped several feet from his truck. He walked toward her.

She'd known he would be as good-looking as his brother. Now beneath fluorescent lights the full impact of Clayton McKinley hit her head-on. He stood two inches over six feet and had a confident, loose-hipped stride. He walked with an easy grace, as though time would wait for him. Lucy had no doubt if he smiled and asked nicely enough it would. Blue jeans clung to him like a second skin and dusty brown boots crunched with defiance over the gravel as he came toward her. His hair was dark blond and cut short on his neck. His eyes were peacock blue and sparkled with a wicked hint of mischief. Clayton McKinley was the kind of man mothers warned their daughters about. The kind fathers had nightmares about. She would always look back on this as one of them. She almost felt like a schoolgirl again. Her palms were suddenly sweaty. Breathing was something she had to think about doing and for the first time in a long time, long dormant emotions began to awaken inside her.

Dragging her eyes away from him she began to shrug out of his jacket, loath to give up the warmth.

"Don't even think about it, lady."

Lucy glared at him as the command rolled seductively off his tongue. "I don't respond well to orders."

"No kidding," he teased, his lips sliding into an easy

smile. Not a generic smile. *Oh, no! This was a knee-weakening, heart-melting, pulse-pounding smile*. This man was dangerous in ways there were no defences for.

"Don't even think of handing the coat back just yet. And arguing with me won't do you any good."

She looked cute swallowed up by his jacket. A small-boned woman, she stirred his protective instincts, and her subtle hourglass shape banished from his mind every stick-thin woman he'd ever dated. Her skin was pale and unblemished, her cheekbones high, her face softly rounded. Her lips were full and naturally pink and had him wondering if they were as sweet as they looked. With her hair pulled into a ponytail she looked about sixteen and more tempting than sin. From the moment she'd turned away in the bar, he'd wondered what colour her eyes were. Now he had his answer. The colour reminded him of fine malt whiskey. They were wide and expressive, guarding a keen intelligence.

Lucy pulled the coat back over her shoulders and tried to ignore the intensity of his watchful gaze. It felt as though he was committing her to memory pore by pore. She refused to be intimidated by his blatant appraisal and motioned to the shop that formed part of the service station.

"I've got to get a few things."

"I'll come with you."

Lucy looked up at him. "You think I'm going to get lost between produce and dairy?"

"I'm having fun." His smile was powerful. His eyes roamed over her from head to toe then made the return journey with lazy intent. Prickles of sensation skittered through her body, skating over nerve endings.

"If grocery shopping is your idea of fun then you

must lead a boring life.'' She said nothing when he fell into step beside her, hands in the pockets of his jeans.

''How did you know Gerry would be at the Roadhouse?''

Lucy entered the shop and picked up a plastic carry basket. She took a loaf of bread from the shelf. ''I didn't. Max said the bloke had a bunch of prissy cowboys—his words not mine—in the car with him. The Roadhouse is the place to be on a Saturday night. I took a chance.''

''Prissy cowboys?'' he repeated, amused. ''Now, if you'd laid that one on Gerry he would have died of embarrassment.''

She took down a box of chocolate pops, putting them into the basket. ''Harrison House is going to be a success.''

''That's what you're calling it?''

She nodded and continued down the aisle. ''We took a vote. The kids decided since Mrs. Harrison's son donated it specifically to be used for the Second Chance project, the name was appropriate. The developers were offering a king's ransom but he didn't want it torn down.''

''Gray Harrison did that for you?''

She met his look with a forthright one of her own. ''Yes, he did. He figured the kids needed something to work for…a goal. Getting the farm up and running again will give them incentive. Gray has been our guardian angel.''

Clayton found it hard to picture Gray Harrison with wings and a halo. Cable Creek had never been big enough for him. He had outgrown the town long before he'd had the means to leave. Now a major player in Australian financial circles, he had a reputation as a ruthless businessman who guarded his private life fiercely.

But none of that mattered to Clayton. All he could think about was what put that soft smile on her face when she spoke the other man's name.

Lucy filled the basket with orange juice, peanut butter and milk before heading for the checkout. When the cashier was finished packing the groceries, Clayton picked up the plastic bag and waited by the door while Lucy paid for both food and fuel. The attendant met them on the way out.

"All done," he said, handing her keys back. Lucy thanked him. Clayton walked her to the car, handing her the bag after she got in behind the wheel. She took it from him with a murmured "thanks" and placed it on the passenger seat. He knelt at her door, his face level with hers.

"Oh, your coat."

"Forget it. I'm following you home."

Lucy glared at him. "I beg your pardon?"

He grinned. "It's on my way and I'd like to know you get there safely."

Did he think she was going to be abducted by aliens between here and there? Lucy bit back the retort. "You don't intend to take money for the fuel, do you, Mr. McKinley?"

"Not for doing the neighbourly thing. And nobody calls me 'mister.' Clayton's fine. But if you really don't want to be in my debt, I'll settle for a cup of coffee."

"I doubt there's anyplace open this time of night, and I noticed the machine in the shop was out of order. Would you take a rain check."

"I'm guessing you own a coffeepot."

"You want coffee...at my house?" She did owe him something for helping her out. He could easily have kept going, leaving her stranded. Lucy wished he would be mercenary and just take her money. "It's well after midnight."

"I'll drink it fast."

"The kids are sleeping."

He shrugged. "I'll be extra quiet."

Subtle wasn't going to work with this man. "I might want to go to bed."

Clayton smiled. "Well, I'm usually not that easy on a first date but I could be persuaded."

Lucy blushed, annoyed as much at herself as him. She'd walked right into that one. "I meant I might want to go to bed...*alone*...to sleep," she said firmly. "And this isn't a date."

He looked as if he'd made a major new discovery. "So that's the other thing people do in bed."

Lucy steeled herself as he smiled again. If he would stop doing that maybe she could concentrate on the conversation and keep herself out of trouble. If she kept this up, she'd be in more hot water than she had ever known.

"One cup, McKinley."

McKinley. Not Clayton. Just McKinley. Polite yet formal. Something that allowed her to keep her distance. Clayton smiled. It would do for now.

"I accept, and remember, I'll be right behind you."

"That's what I'm afraid of," she muttered to herself. She watched in the rearview mirror, studying his compact backside with female appreciation as he walked away. One cup of coffee, she told herself. Then he would leave, if she had to push his gorgeous body and that come-get-me grin out the door.

Chapter Two

At the house he met her on the veranda steps. Once inside she left the groceries on the couch and excused herself to go check on Max. Clayton was left to close the door behind him. He took off his hat, almost able to hear Mrs. Harrison reprimanding him for such a breach of etiquette in her home. This house was like an old friend. He hadn't been inside in years but the memories came flooding back. The sleepovers and camping trips. The fishing expeditions and the carefree weekends spent helping Gray's grandfather build the tree house in the backyard. Those days seemed a lifetime ago now.

Lucy came back downstairs, her jaw clenched.

"Everything okay?"

"I'd like to take a two-by-four to Gerry Anderson's skull, though I doubt it would even leave an impression." The warmth of the house reminded Lucy that she still wore his coat. She shrugged out of it. "Thanks for the loan."

"Any time." Clayton took it from her, making sure

his fingers brushed over hers. Lucy looked up, her eyes wide and wary. A reaction was all he'd wanted. He laid the coat over the arm of the couch, inhaling the light, flowery fragrance that clung to it. He sat his hat on top. "It's a beautiful old house."

Fine. If he wasn't going to mention the last few seconds, neither would she. He'd taken her by surprise but she wouldn't let it happen again. "The hardwood floors need sanding, then I'll polish. The wallpaper in some rooms needs replacing and the whole structure needs a coat of weatherproof paint." The house had stood idle for the last two years. The large living room had boxes still stacked in a corner waiting to be emptied. "I think we're going to be very happy here." She picked up the sack of groceries. "I'll put the coffee on."

Clayton followed her into the kitchen and made himself comfortable on a straight-backed chair at the table. The room was inviting. The pale lemon of the freshly painted walls blended nicely with the brand-new light grey linoleum on the floor. While the coffee perked, Lucy set out ceramic mugs on the counter. She went to the refrigerator and withdrew a container. "Chocolate cake?"

"Thanks."

She sliced two pieces of cake with medical precision and set them on plates. When she paused to lick a dab of chocolate icing from her finger, he couldn't look away. He couldn't do much of anything! The only basic function he maintained was breathing…but only with a concentrated effort. Her lips closed around her finger back to the first knuckle. She pulled it out of her mouth so slowly he almost groaned. She broke the spell by placing the knife in the sink and the cake back in the refrigerator. Clayton shifted in his chair to relieve the beginnings of arousal.

The coffee was finally done and she busied herself placing forks, milk and sugar on the table. She set cake and coffee before him, then went back for her own, carrying a can in the crook of her elbow when she sat down opposite him at the table.

"Whipped cream?" he asked. "I thought all you city people were health nuts. Low-fat this, high-fibre that."

She shook the can vigorously before squirting a quantity onto her cake. "Not me. There are some things I won't give up even for the sake of my arteries."

"Such as?"

She thought about it for a few seconds. "Hamburgers, pizza, potato chips...whipped cream. The kids say my eating habits are going to kill me some day but hey, why not die happy?"

She could eat junk food and still have a body like that? The look of absolute anticipation on her face mesmerized him. Her delicate pink tongue peeked between perfect teeth as she concentrated on sculpting a work of art with the cream. Lucy paused, her fork in midair. "You have a strange look on your face."

Clayton figured it was a little too soon in their relationship to divulge that watching her smooth whipped cream onto a piece of chocolate cake had aroused him. He didn't want her thinking he was some kind of pervert.

"I've never seen anyone look at a piece of cake like it was a three-course meal."

"Yeah, well, I skipped lunch because tonight is pizza night and that's better than sex. But then Max came home and I took him to the doctor, I got so upset, the last thing on my mind was food. Now I'm starving."

Better than sex? In Clayton's experience there weren't

many things that even came close to the delicious euphoria of sex.

"Are you saying that you'd rather have pizza than sex?" If that was the case then she hadn't found the right partner. He was already preparing his application for the position. *Fun-loving farmer seeks to warm the bed of prickly little cactus flower. Satisfaction guaranteed every time.*

Lucy had given too many safe-sex lectures to streetwise teens to be easily embarrassed, though she wished he weren't studying her so intently. "You make it sound like nothing could possibly be better."

"Good sex is pretty tough to top. Two people wanting each other so badly that nothing else matters but the moment," he said, his gaze dropping to her lips. "A deep-pan cheesy crust with everything doesn't even come close."

"At least with a pizza you can order ahead, have it delivered, know what you're getting, and if it isn't satisfying you can take it back and get a refund." With a serene smile that she hoped would effectively end the conversation, she raised the laden fork to her mouth.

Clayton watched her lips close around the fork, gliding along the tines as her eyes closed. He'd eaten meals with a lot of women in his thirty years. But this woman turned eating into one of the most erotic things he'd ever witnessed. Clayton didn't question the urge he had to lean over and taste the sweetness of cake and cream on her mouth. Nor did he act on it...not just yet. He looked away long enough to get his body back under some sense of control before attacking his own cake.

"How long have you worked with these kids?"

Lucy stirred her coffee. "Five years."

He smiled. "Not real big on details, are you?"

Lucy raised an eyebrow at him. "That would depend on the topic of discussion."

He pointed to her with his fork. "You."

"Then it's going to be a very short conversation."

The expression on her face dared him to try to prove her wrong. Normally he didn't back down from a dare, but he sensed a need to go carefully with her. "So, how do you like your pizza?"

Lucy looked up at him, momentarily startled by the abrupt topic change, and wondered if this was a double-edged sword, given their previous conversation about pizza and sex. "With everything," she said. "Is there any other way to have it?"

"Cold."

"God, that's disgusting!"

Okay. So I'll never suggest we have cold pizza for breakfast, he thought wryly.

"The one food you couldn't do without?"

Lucy didn't even hesitate. "Seafood…any and all."

He filed it away for future reference.

"What's going on?"

Clayton looked up. The girl standing in the doorway was in her late teens. She wore pajamas that hung on her thin frame, her long black hair streaked a startling white-blond in places. He wasn't sure what the nose ring and the black nail polish were in aid of, but despite them she was a very pretty girl.

"Sorry if we woke you, Lisa."

She stifled a yawn. "No. I've been awake on and off since you left," she said, sparing Clayton a glance.

"Coffee's hot."

Lisa looked over at the pot as if it were booby-trapped. "Did you make it?"

Lucy sighed. "Yes, I did."

"I'll pass. One medical emergency a day is all you can handle." She sat down beside Lucy, casting a wary glance at Clayton before looking at her. "You should have taken me with you."

Lucy smiled and shook her head. "I needed you here to keep Max calm. You're the only one who can sweet-talk him."

"I just let her think she can," said the boy in question, coming into the kitchen, his curly blond hair tousled, his eyes sleepy. "I ache all over, Lucy. I hope you knocked him on his fat old butt."

Clayton grinned at the sentiment as Lucy fussed over Max, but one look at the boy when he turned around, wearing nothing but bright red shorts, and he was tempted to go find Gerry Anderson and administer a dose of the man's own medicine. A bruise covered one side of Max's face. His thin body bore the evidence of his fall. Ugly purple cuts, painful-looking scratches and skin scraped raw. Behind Max two more kids ambled in. The oldest, a dark-haired boy, teetered on the brink of manhood and adopted the stance of a warrior. He was a born survivor. It was in his eyes. The girl standing beside him was younger than Lisa—about fourteen. Her hair was long and red, her smile infectious.

"This is Clayton McKinley. He's our neighbour from Cable Downs," Lucy said by way of introduction.

Thomas narrowed his intense glare on Clayton.

"We didn't mean to wake everyone. Coffee's hot, Thomas."

He looked suspicious. "Who made it?"

Lucy made an aggrieved sound. "I made the darn coffee. Besides, McKinley's drinking it and he hasn't keeled over yet."

Thomas shrugged. "It don't mean he won't."

Actually Clayton had yet to taste the coffee she'd made him. He'd tasted bad coffee before. He'd tasted coffee so strong it could anaesthetize a bull at fifty paces. Now he eyed the cup wondering just how bad Lucy's brew was.

"You're quite safe, McKinley," she said, interpreting his look. "I haven't killed anybody yet."

Thomas scoffed. "The way you make coffee it's just a matter of time."

The redhead swatted him playfully on the arm. "Leave Lucy alone." Then she smiled at Clayton. "I'm Katie." She gave Lucy a pointed look. "He's cute. How about you tie him to your bed and keep him?"

Clayton nearly choked on the mouthful of cake he'd just eaten, and Lucy felt a perverse sense of satisfaction. After having him throw her off balance more than once tonight, turnabout was proving highly entertaining.

"I don't collect men like stray animals, Katie. We met tonight. The car ran out of petrol on the highway and McKinley was kind enough to help me out."

Thomas pulled out a chair beside Clayton and plonked into it. "Did you find the guy?" he asked Lucy.

"I found him," she said. "I handled the whole situation rationally and calmly just the way it needed to be."

Clayton chuckled and Lucy shot him a warning look to keep his mouth shut, which he promptly ignored.

"I've seen rational," he told her. "And I've seen calm. But walking into a bar and challenging a guy twice your size in front of all his friends doesn't qualify as either, Lucy." He looked her straight in the eye. "You showed more guts than a lot of men I know."

Thomas straightened as if he'd been shot and glared at Clayton. "She did that? You were there?"

Clayton nodded. "You would have been proud of

her.'' He glanced across at Lucy, who looked fit to strangle him. ''She might be small, but there's nothing tiny about her temper.''

Katie hoisted herself onto the waist-high breakfast bar. ''Did you at least punch him out or kick him you-know-where?'' At the look Clayton gave her, she added, ''Lucy knows self-defence.''

Clayton could have sworn there was a thinly veiled warning in there. He smiled. ''I know. She took lessons a while back.''

Thomas glared at her. ''You walked in there with no one at your back? That's the quickest way there is to wind up dead.''

Lucy knew she'd allowed her anger to cloud her judgement and she'd put herself in a dangerous position. She had to be more careful. Her family needed her.

''You're right, Thomas. I shouldn't have gone alone.''

Thomas shifted uncomfortably in his chair.

''Yeah, well,'' he said, looking embarrassed at his display of concern. ''Don't go doing it again, okay? Any creep who'd hurt a kid as small as Max wouldn't be afraid of taking on a woman.''

''Hey, I'm not small,'' Max grumbled, wiping his eyes while avoiding the bruises. Clayton noticed now that his lip was cut too. ''I'll get bigger...but I don't want to ride anymore.''

Clayton cautiously sipped the coffee while Lucy was fussing over Max. After the first taste, he placed the mug back on the table, forcing the liquid down his throat. Lucy's coffee wasn't bad. It was toxic. He heaped four sugars into it hoping it might at least make the stuff palatable.

''Where did you get the horse?''

''Col Peterson sold me three.'' Lucy stroked Max's

head. "Give it a few days until the soreness goes away, sweetie, and then you can take her out again."

The boy shook his head emphatically. Clayton had been around horses since before he could talk and had been riding them—albeit in his father's arms—since before he'd taken his first steps.

"School doesn't start back for another week," Clayton said, "so anytime you want to come over to the Downs we could use another hand." And maybe he could coax this kid not to give up on horse riding just yet. He'd let the fear recede first and then see what happened.

"Do you have jillaroos?" asked Katie, her excitement barely contained. "Everything is equal opportunity now, you know."

Clayton hid a smile. "I don't have a problem with that. You'll find as many women doing farm labouring as there are men. In fact, we have three regular shed hands who hire on each year for shearing and they're female."

Katie's eyes widened. "How about it, Lucy?"

Lucy didn't really have a choice. Clayton McKinley had put the idea out there guessing she would never deny the kids the opportunity. If she had to have the kids learning from anyone, it might as well be him.

"All right, you can do it."

"Sounds like I just hired myself two more hands." He looked to Thomas and then to Lisa. "The invitation to visit is extended to all of you." Thomas nodded slowly. Lisa shrugged.

"When you said hired, did you mean as in paid?"

"Max!" Lucy cast an apologetic look at her guest.

Clayton smiled. "All our hands get paid, even our part-timers."

"No, McKinley, you've done—"

"Nothing more than hire extra hands to help around the farm. We've got fences to mend, stock to move and crops to finish harvesting, if they don't get washed away first. I've got three orphaned lambs and no doubt we'll have more before lambing season is over. Then there's always the stables to muck out."

Clayton could afford to pay these kids for the work they would do. He remembered how proud he'd felt when his after-school job had earned him enough money to buy the bike he'd wanted one year. Their eagerness told him he wouldn't be disappointed. Of course, the fact that it would give him an excuse to see Lucy on a regular basis was just a fringe benefit.

"Lambs?" Katie's eyes sparkled with excitement. "Cool. I've never seen one up close."

Max grinned, wincing slightly because of his split lip. "You want to see one up close, look at your hamburger the next time you eat one."

"That's beef," she replied smugly, "And stop being so gross." She looked at Clayton. "When do we start?"

"Tomorrow, if it's okay with Lucy."

Yeah, right, she thought. *Now he defers to my opinion when he's all but given them a bed and three square meals a day!* Neighbourly or not she wasn't just going to let him steamroll into her life and turn it upside down.

Katie smiled at Lucy's nod. "What time?"

"I'm usually up and at it by about six."

Max gulped. "In the morning?"

Katie's bright smile faltered for the first time. "Are you out of your mind? The sun isn't even up then."

Lucy chuckled. "How would you know? You're never awake that early."

Katie looked horrified that it might actually be true. "I'm guessing."

Clayton bit back a smile. "I'll meet you at the house at ten." Their relief was almost comical.

"Enough, back to bed everyone," said Lucy.

Thomas glanced at Clayton then back to Lucy. "You'll be okay?"

Touched by his concern, she smiled. "Of course. McKinley and I need to talk about a few things."

Katie gave Clayton an assessing look. "See you in the morning…boss." She tugged at Thomas's hand and they followed Max out of the kitchen.

"Why did you offer them jobs?" Lucy asked as soon as the kids were gone.

Clayton sat back in his chair. "Lady, you bring new meaning to the word *suspicious*."

"Compliments won't get you anywhere, now answer the question."

"You probably think I did it so I could get close to you."

"Did you?"

He cursed softly and brutally mashed a piece of cake with his fork, looking back at her when he felt more in control. She stared at him with assessing eyes. "What I did here tonight I did for those kids. Not only can I keep them busy but they might learn a thing or two. I may even get Max over his fear of horses. They'll never be idle, that's for sure."

"I don't want them hurt."

"I'll keep an eye on them, make sure they stay out of mischief."

"I meant emotionally." She sipped her coffee. "What Gerry said tonight, about the kids being strays. I don't want them to hear people saying those things," she said, reining in her anger. "They deserve a chance. They need to be accepted."

Her words touched him, the strength in them, the fire in her eyes. Did these kids know how much they were loved? he wondered.

"They won't hear any of that garbage over at Cable Downs. I only have four men on the payroll and they're all good blokes. Once I introduce the kids, the men know to act accordingly."

Lucy wished he didn't sound so sincere. It just made it more difficult not to like him. And Lucy was determined not to like him. Neighbourliness was one thing, but liking opened up a whole other can of worms that Lucy knew should stay very firmly closed. She emptied her cup and looked over at his. "Finished?"

Clayton grinned. "Is that your subtle way of telling me it's time I was going?"

She raised an imperious eyebrow, trying to ignore what that smile did to her insides. "If subtle worked with you I would be upstairs asleep and you wouldn't be here."

He feigned a wounded look. "You mean to say you'd send me out on a night like this with just one cup of coffee under my belt?"

And that tack wouldn't persuade her either. "Thomas would say I was doing you a favour."

Truth be told she was right. After that one mouthful, he wasn't expecting to get any sleep tonight. How the hell he was going to finish the whole lot he didn't know. But he thought of it as a test. Though he'd like to know what she used to put the coffee in the percolator. He was guessing garden spade. A large one. He looked down at his plate and then back to her, grinning. "I've got cake left."

Lucy sat back, hoping for that bored, unaffected look Lisa did so well. "Then I suggest you eat it."

Oh, he would. The cake was world-class compared to the coffee. He waved his fork in her direction. "Give me a chance, Lucy. I'll grow on you."

Give him a chance? Not if she had one ounce of self-preservation in her body! "I don't even know you."

His gaze pinned her with undeniable challenge. He aimed to change that as soon as possible. "What do you mean you don't know me? I help damsels in distress, children like me...and I drink your coffee. I think that last one should qualify me for some kind of bravery award. What more do you need to know?"

How to get you out of my life before you become a complication I can't afford, she thought ruefully. "You haven't finished the coffee yet," she reminded him smugly. "And what do you mean bravery award?" She frowned. "Are you saying my coffee's lousy?"

"Of course not." And he wasn't lying. It left lousy in the dust. Lousy gave the impression it could be improved. Clayton doubted anything short of an exorcism could make her coffee fit for general human consumption.

"It's getting late," she pointed out.

Clayton grinned. "I've got an idea."

"What you've got is a hide thicker than any rhinoceros."

He smiled again and this time she couldn't muster a defence for it. She had to get him out of her kitchen, out of her house...and then she had to avoid him as much as possible. Either that or try to forget he was the reason they put the S in sinful.

"I've never had any complaints about the state of my hide, Lucy. I think you should wait until you have first-

hand knowledge of it before you make rash statements.''
He smiled as he purposely reached for the mug and
drank the coffee. He hoped his medical insurance was
up to date. How much did a stomach pump cost? he
wondered.

Lucy leaned her arms on the table and met his gaze
with a direct one of her own as he put the mug back on
the table and finished off his cake. This was something
they needed to get out of the way right now. "We're
neighbours. You're helping the kids to feel more at home
here and I appreciate it, but we are never going to be
more than that.''

So, she could tell he was interested. That was a good
start. "Never is a long time, Lucy. Are you sure you
don't want to renegotiate the time frame?''

She stood up. "Go home." He put the fork on the
plate along with his mug then pushed to his feet, still
grinning as if he was having the time of his life.
Great…just great! That was definitely the combination
she needed in a man. Drop-dead sexy, lethally charming
and annoyingly persistent.

"Don't you want to know my idea?''

Lucy scowled. "Do I get a choice?''

"No.''

She glared at him. "Fine, as long as it gets you out
of my house." His smile wasn't triumphant enough to
be a smirk but it came darn close.

"Do you ride?''

Lucy didn't trust his casual tone. She just knew there
was a trapdoor here somewhere. She hoped she saw it
before it was too late. "Horses?''

He chuckled. "We'd better stick to livestock or this
conversation could take on a whole new meaning.''

Too late! She'd have to watch for the next potential slip. "No, I don't ride horses."

"Then I'll teach you."

"I didn't say I didn't know how to ride a horse. I just said I didn't ride them."

"Well, can you ride?"

She folded her arms and wondered if she really would have to push him out the door. "No."

"Then I'll give you lessons."

Oh, I'll just bet you could, Clayton McKinley. "What you'll give me is a mitigating circumstance for homicide," she said, exasperated and not totally immune to the fact that he was flirting with her. "As for the lessons, I don't think so. The farther off the ground you are, the more it hurts when you fall off."

"What if I promise to catch you?"

Oh, that was a much better idea. Hitting the ground would be less dangerous. "My answer would be the same."

Clayton would have fun changing her mind. "I'd better be going. Thanks for the coffee and cake."

"Thank you for the assistance." Lucy followed him out of the kitchen and through the living room, where he picked up his coat and hat before heading out the door. He turned on the threshold, meeting her gaze. "I'll see you when you drop the kids off tomorrow."

"I have some things to do in the morning. I'll get Thomas to drive them over."

Clayton smiled. "Are you afraid of me?"

Lucy trembled involuntarily as that low, soft drawl skittered up her spine. With a momentum of its own it radiated to all points of her body. She raised her chin and tried to ignore the sensation, meeting his steady gaze with what she hoped was a withering glare.

"In your dreams."

"You will be," he replied easily. "I'm going to be seeing a lot more of you, Lucy Warner." He reached out and soft as a whisper stroked the back of his fingers down her cheek, mesmerized by the softness he met and by the way she became immobile with...what was that in her eyes? Panic? Fear? He pulled his hand away, realizing he would have to go slower with this woman that he ever had in his life. He put his hat on and shrugged into his coat.

"It doesn't matter if you hide out here and try to avoid me, Lucy. We're going to be good together. That is a promise and a McKinley always keeps his promises."

Lucy couldn't look away from him, couldn't forget the feelings his fingers had elicited. She raised her chin a notch and looked him straight in the eye. "You think I can't resist you?"

He tucked his thumbs into the belt hooks of his jeans. "I think I'd like you to try. Sounds like it might be fun." Then he turned serious. "And one more thing. I would never hurt those kids to get close to you. I plan to do that all by myself."

Lucy shivered but it had nothing to do with the night air and everything to do with the man who threatened to thaw her heart with just a sexy smile. He turned and walked down the steps, the porch light illuminating the path to his truck.

"I'm not getting involved with you." It had seemed important to get that out in the open so there could be no misunderstandings. But when he turned and looked back at her, one hand on the door of the vehicle, Lucy realized how well this man played the game.

"I'll make a bet with you that we'll be dining over candlelight before next Saturday."

Lucy crossed her arms and leaned back on the doorframe, hiding a small smile at his tenacity. "And when you lose that wager, what do I get?"

He didn't miss a beat. "If I lose, you'll get the satisfaction of seeing me fall flat on my backside and an extra pair of hands to help you scrape down this house. But I intend to win, Lucy, and when I do, my payment will be giving you those riding lessons you need...and a kiss."

Lucy considered herself unshockable after so many years spent around kids for whom shock value had its own rewards, but his suggestion almost caught her off guard. Kissing Clayton McKinley was not a good idea. Just the touch of his finger on her cheek had almost curled her toes...and her toes didn't curl for anyone!

"It's a deal."

He touched the rim of his hat and gave her another one of those dangerous smiles. "Yeah, it's a deal. But it's going to be a pleasure, Lucy. You can count on that."

She stood there and watched him drive off into the night, waiting until she could no longer see his taillights in the distance.

Clayton McKinley had stirred her libido to life again as easily as he breathed. And Lucy was scared. Not because of his striking good looks, not even because of his laid-back charm. But because she'd known the man less than two hours and feelings were waking inside her. He'd stroked her cheek and her insides quivered. He smiled and she could almost hear the barricade around her emotions straining under the force of it. She had never felt anything so consuming and that was her fear.

How could she protect herself from something she couldn't control? Lucy had a feeling she'd just let a major complication into her life.

How much damage he did would be up to her.

Chapter Three

If he was surprised the next morning when she drove her car into the driveway of Cable Downs, he didn't show it. In fact, he looked downright pleased with himself. The kids wasted no time getting out, though Max was stiff and sore from his injuries and Katie tried to act as if this whole thing was no big deal, when they all knew otherwise.

Lucy followed after a moment or two in which she got her racing heartbeat back under some semblance of control. He'd been hard at it already. Sweat and dust clung to the thin cotton T-shirt that stretched across his chest and shoulders. He was potent. Masculine. Rugged. A down-home original.

Clayton touched the rim of his hat and smiled at Lucy before turning his attention to the kids. "I've got hats and sunscreen for both of you up in the house. And it's good to see you wore sensible shoes. I reckon I'll make farmers out of you yet."

Lucy watched them bask in his praise. No matter how

she felt about Clayton, this would be good for Max and Katie. They'd been dreading the holidays. Soon enough their farm would be up and running, though not on the grand scale of this one. Until then, the chores were boring, repetitive and uninteresting.

"Go on up to the house," he said, "and you'll get morning tea before we head out."

They didn't need to be told twice, and when they were gone, Clayton stood face-to-face with the woman who had haunted what little sleep he had managed last night. "So I guess you're not afraid of me after all."

If he weren't so darn charming his words would have almost been arrogant. "I wouldn't have taken the bet if I was afraid of you." He smiled and Lucy didn't even try to shield herself from the effect, taking it as a given when a shiver skittered down her spine.

"Walk with me up to the house before all the goodies disappear with the hungry hordes," he said, leading the way to the large homestead with its low-slung veranda and jasmine vines clinging to the railing. "I didn't think you'd go for that bet, but you surprised me."

"I know I'm going to win."

Clayton smiled, wondering if he would ever get to see her in anything but jeans. She had a lemon-coloured sweatshirt on today and a pair of worn boots. Granted, she did things to a pair of jeans that would give a corpse palpitations, but he'd wager those legs would look dynamite in a skirt.

"Confidence. I like that in a woman. I find it sexy. You know, wondering if it spills over into other facets of her life."

His smile had Lucy thinking of crisp cool sheets and Clayton...a combination that would get her in deep trouble, fantasy or not. "Just so we don't get our signals crossed, are you flirting with me, McKinley?"

He took off his hat as he approached the veranda steps. Damp hair clung to his forehead and he reached up to brush it back with a smooth, long-fingered stroke. "I believe that's what they call it," he replied, not the least bit bashful. "Flirting is the basis of any good seduction."

Lucy took a deep breath. Why couldn't he just beat around the bush now and again without always having to just come right out with what he was thinking?

"You can't seduce me."

"Oh, it might take a while, since you're not quite sure what my motives are...or whether you can trust me," he said, never once breaking eye contact with her. "But it will happen."

"I'm not attracted to you," she said, wanting it to be true. His expression told her he knew otherwise and darn it if he wasn't right.

"Then you've got nothing to worry about."

"That's right, I've had a vaccination to protect me from charming men."

Clayton raised a dark eyebrow at her. "You think I'm charming?"

Loath as she was to admit it, Lucy knew there was no use denying it. "At the risk of encouraging you, any red-blooded woman would find you charming." His soft smile sent a spiral of heat through her body.

"But I don't want just any red-blooded woman...I want you."

Lucy might be one hundred percent shockproof but she still wasn't immune to a sexy man saying those words to her, looking at her with unmistakable desire.

No man had ever desired her. But she could see it in his eyes. *Attraction.* She felt it all the way to her bones.

"Does the word *subtle* have any significance for you?" she said. "You can't just go around saying whatever's on your mind."

He shrugged. "Seems to me it saves time and confusion. Have dinner with me," he said, changing gears again. "Tonight. In town."

Lucy chuckled. He got full marks for persistence. "You think I'm going to make it that easy?"

"Lord, I hope not. That would take all the fun out of it."

Lucy bit back a smile. "I meant it won't be that easy to catch me out and win the bet by inviting me to some candlelit restaurant."

Clayton held the door open for her. "You'll say yes to me, eventually."

And she wondered if that was another McKinley promise he intended to keep. Inside she didn't get much of a chance to do more than nod politely to the four men who sat around the oblong-shaped wooden table in the kitchen. No sooner had Clayton introduced her to Shay Hamilton, ranch housekeeper and family friend, and the farmhands than the men were plucking hats off the rack in the corner and heading back out to work.

Shay looked across at her. "Coffee?"

Lucy smiled. "Thanks."

"Boss, me and Charlie will keep going on that other section of downed fence."

Clayton poured himself a cup of coffee. "Okay, Bob. We should finish it in case that predicted storm blows in. I'll be down in a few minutes. Harry, you and Derek keep going on the combine so it'll be ready when that part comes in this afternoon."

The tall, red-haired man nodded. "Real nice scones, Shay."

"Thank you, Harry."

Lucy watched the young auburn-haired woman fuss over Max and Katie, who both milked the attention for all they were worth. They questioned Clayton about everything from what kind of animals he had apart from sheep, to what they might be doing all day. Clayton mentioned they had a pig that was pretty close to giving birth and Katie was in heaven. Max, on the other hand, seemed more interested in what a combine was.

"Will we get to see any cowboys?" asked Max, sipping his milk.

Shay chuckled and Clayton smiled broadly. "The blokes that work the sheep and cattle aren't called cowboys, they're called ringers," he told Max.

"Except Clem," said Shay, coming to sit beside Max. "He's what's known as a roustabout. He used to be a ringer but now that he's older he has other chores."

Katie reached for another scone. "Like what?"

"He makes certain we've got fresh milk every morning, he tends the chickens that give us our free-range eggs and he's an expert at slaughtering meat for us. He also does the gardening, but he insists he doesn't enjoy it."

Max grinned. "Wow! You eat your own animals?"

Clayton spread preserves on a scone and looked across at him. "It's no different to going to the supermarket and buying it in those little plastic-wrapped trays."

Katie cast a wary glance at Lucy. "Tell me we won't be eating any of our animals when we get the farm up and running."

Lucy smiled. The kids were certainly going to get an

education working here. "When we get the fences fixed and so forth, we'll probably try keeping animals...but I think we'll start off small and raise them to sell."

Katie turned a questioned glance at Clayton. "What about the piglets when they're born? Do you...eat them too?"

Lucy had a fair idea of where this conversation was headed. Given her way, the girl would have two of every animal sleeping in her room! Even before Lucy could intervene, Clayton preempted her.

"We have about three dozen. Some are used for meat, some are kept for breeding, but most we sell at market."

"If I saved my money, could I buy one off you?"

"I guess you'll have to talk it over with Lucy."

Katie looked at her expectantly. "Can I, Lucy?"

"Maybe when we have somewhere to put it."

Max grinned mischievously. "You'd better let her have one, Lucy, otherwise the next time she sees it, she could be eating it with eggs and toast."

Katie looked across at Lucy. "Do boys ever stop being irritating?"

Lucy looked at Shay, who seemed amused by the question. "No," they chorused in unison, both chuckling at the look of mock disgust Clayton sent their way.

"Max, my boy, we'd better get out of here. I'm beginning to feel like a duck in hunting season," he said, scooping his hat off the rack. "You ready, Katie?"

She wasn't, but in three seconds flat the glass of milk was gone and she was following behind him. He touched his hat. "I'll be seeing you again, Lucy."

"No doubt. You do have my kids."

"That's not what I was talking about and you know it." Then he was gone.

"Good grief! Maybe I should get the hose."

Shay's statement caught Lucy off guard. "I beg your pardon?"

"The hose. With the look he gave you just then I'm surprised you're not going up in flames."

Lucy took a sip of coffee. "Really? I'm surprised I haven't murdered him."

"Already? It usually takes women a little longer to realize how persistent he is!"

"Well, there's persistent and then there's annoying."

"When he walked out of here you looked like you didn't know whether to kiss him or strangle him." Shay laughed and shook her head. "He likes you."

Lucy shifted uncomfortably in her chair. "I get the feeling he likes women in general…and it wouldn't be a stretch of the imagination to see them liking him even more."

Shay sat down across the table from her. "I've known him for a long time, and I've never seen a woman who didn't fall for him just a little when she met him."

Oh, Lucy could believe that. The man was breathing. To attract women he wouldn't have to do much else.

Shay smiled. "He's just got…something. They all have it in some way but Clayton just knows how to work it."

And Lucy knew she would be a millionaire if she could bottle and market Clayton's particular brand of something.

"He's hard not to like," she admitted. "And gorgeous with it, but I'm not falling for his charm."

"Don't be so sure," said Shay, shaking her head. "Once Clayton sets his sights on something, he's the most determined man I've ever seen. Nothing distracts him."

"Then irresistible force is about to meet immovable

object,'' said Lucy, wondering if she was up to the task of resisting him. "I've got the children to think about."

Shay nodded solemnly. "I heard what happened last night. Poor Max, he still looks so sore. Someone needs to knock that spiteful streak out of Gerry Anderson." Then she smiled. "Just remember, Clayton's one of the good guys."

"And irritating."

"Only now and again. That's a McKinley trait. It's genetic. They all suffer from it in differing degrees."

Lucy frowned, curiosity getting the better of her. "How long have you known the McKinleys?"

"Twelve years. Our fathers were roughriders on the rodeo circuit and became good friends. Eventually Walt McKinley gave it up to get married and offered my dad a job as foreman." She smiled in remembrance. "Poor Les didn't even know I existed until the summer Walt's wife died. My mum dumped me here and took off for God knows where," she said. "All of a sudden I had a dad, three surrogate brothers, and when I hit my teens, not much of a social life to speak of."

"How do you keep the three of them in line?"

Shay grinned and held up her hands in a "search me" gesture. "Dumb luck, I think."

"You've never thought of living in town?"

Shay shook her head, but there was something in her expression that Lucy couldn't pin down, something so quick it was as if it had never existed.

"Someone has to take care of them and I'd miss Molly— She's Josh's daughter, and since he's raising her alone, she needs a woman around. Besides, this is the only place I've ever really called home. I have family, my part-time job at the Roadhouse and fresh country air," she said. "To a kid who got dragged from one

town to the next by her mother for the first ten years of
her life, being settled is a dream come true.'' She met
Lucy's curious frown. ''Rita was a barrel racer, that's
how she met my father. We followed the rodeos wherever they went.''

They talked for the next half hour and Lucy learned
more about this pretty, quietly spoken woman. She'd
turned twenty-one just last month and her father had died
four years earlier after a long battle with cancer. She
was happy with her life, content in a way few people
ever knew. Lucy was sure she'd ever known contentment. Since the age of sixteen she'd gone through life
with blinders on, not allowing anything to distract her.
She had learned the hard way that distractions came at
a price.

Lucy made it into town for painting supplies an hour
later and spent the rest of the day scraping the yellowed
wallpaper from the rooms upstairs. Thomas began scraping the outside of the house and Lisa started washing
down the walls in her room, her music playing loud
enough to wake the dead.

As she worked, Lucy envisaged what this place would
look like in a month or two. They would have chickens.
The pen was already built. Possibly a handful of sheep
and maybe a cow or two. And if Katie got her way, no
doubt they would have a few lambs and a pig to add to
the menagerie. Max had asked for a rabbit of his own
for his birthday, and Thomas, well, he'd taken to feeding
the stray tomcat that had been hanging around the house
since their arrival. She'd never thought of Thomas as a
cat person, but the animal followed him around wherever
he went on the farm...and hissed at the rest of them.

Cowardly or not, she sent Thomas to fetch Katie and

Max that afternoon. Lucy wanted to get dinner on the table and soak in the big old, claw-footed bathtub upstairs, and she wanted some time to marshal her defences against the charms of Clayton McKinley. She was peeling vegetables when they arrived home, bursting into the kitchen excitedly.

"We met Clayton's other brother, Zach!" Katie exclaimed, carrying her hat with care. "And Josh's little girl."

Lucy sliced the carrots. "Sounds like you had fun," she replied. "Did you learn anything?"

"Clayton told me how they bring in a crop," said Max, beaming despite the bruises to his face that were beginning to darken. If Lucy wasn't mistaken, a serious case of hero worship had been born.

"And I learned that mucking out stalls over there is pretty much the same as mucking out stalls right here, only they have more horses and I'm getting paid for it," said Katie, wrinkling her nose and grinning.

"Keep up with that attitude, sweetie, and you'll be a millionaire before you're thirty," said Lucy, kissing Katie's forehead. "Go feed the animals then wash up for dinner and you can tell me all about it."

Lucy watched out the kitchen window as one by one the pets were fed and housed for the night. Barnaby never liked going back in his cage and it usually took Katie at least five minutes to coax the wily rabbit to the point where she could catch him, then she moved on to put feed and fresh water in Sylvester's cage. The ferret didn't like Lucy and that was just fine because Lucy wasn't overenamoured of the rodent either, no matter how cute and harmless Katie tried to tell her it was.

Max, meanwhile, fed his ducks and the three guinea pigs that were his pride and joy.

When they sat down to dinner, Lucy sat back and listened, enjoying their happiness.

Lucy managed to avoid Clayton for three whole days, though she had a nagging suspicion it was only because he wanted it that way. It was like trying to second-guess the mind of some diabolical madman, wondering what he would do next. A very sexy, very tempting madman. She'd arrived after dinner to pick the kids up Thursday evening. It was Shay who opened the door to her.

"Sorry I'm late."

But Shay waved away her concerns and assured her feeding the teens hadn't taken any extra effort. They walked into the kitchen and the sight that greeted her spoke of one thing…home. The kind of home she wanted for her kids and all those who would follow. A tight fist of long-dormant emotion stirred. At the table they sat, talking and laughing. Clayton, Max and Katie were on one side, Josh and the child she knew must be Molly seated across from them. Shay introduced the dark-haired, thoughtful-looking man at the head of the table as the oldest McKinley brother, Zach. According to the children, he had taken over the business side of the farm when their father died and was a whiz with computers. He preferred managing the breeding and bookkeeping part of Cable Downs, though often he got in and worked side by side with Clayton.

"Take a load off. You look exhausted," said Clayton, accompanying the request with a smile so scorching she was surprised the leather on the soles of her boots hadn't started to smoulder. He looked good, not a speck of dust anywhere on him, his hair damp and unruly. She wondered if he knew what his smile did to her, then decided she probably didn't want to know.

Lucy pulled out a chair beside Josh and sat down. "Scraping wallpaper all day will do that to you."

From up the table Molly waggled her fingers at Lucy and smiled. "Are you married?"

Josh looked at his daughter. "That's not polite, Molly."

"It's all right." Lucy didn't dare look around her at the faces of the others. "No, I'm not married."

"Uncle Clayton thinks you're pretty."

Lucy wondered what the odds were of an earthquake cracking the ground wide open so she could crawl in. She could feel Clayton's eyes on her but she didn't dare look across at him. Zach sighed, Josh shot Lucy an apologetic look and Shay hid a smile. Max and Katie giggled.

"That's enough, Molly."

The child looked up at her father. "But Uncle Clayton said it, Daddy, so why can't I tell Lucy?"

"Because you're embarrassing her."

Molly looked down the table at her. "Are you 'barrassed, Lucy?"

"Every woman likes to be told she's pretty," she said, avoiding the question. "I'll bet your Uncle Clayton tells you all the time how pretty you are."

"Yep. I'm the prettiest six-year-old he knows." Molly smiled at Clayton and he winked back then he looked directly at Lucy. She knew looking away, avoiding his gaze was not only smart but necessary for her survival. Yet his lips slowly slid into a smile that kick-started her heart and made her palms sweat. His gaze dropped just a fraction and she could tell he was looking at her mouth. Was he thinking about kissing her? God knew she had thought enough about kissing him. He'd obviously been talking to his family about her. There was no escaping the hold this man had on her senses…on her.

"Here you go, you look like you could do with this," said Shay, placing a steaming mug of coffee in front of her and a comforting hand on her shoulder. "I'll get you some apple pie. Unless you'd like dinner?"

"Pie will be fine," she said, feeling bad about taking that. "Don't go to any trouble on my account."

"Nonsense. I've just fed this lot. Getting you something won't kill me. And since you've just passed the junior version of the McKinley inquisition, I'd say you've earned it."

"How's the car, Lucy?" asked Max. "Clayton said you had trouble with it."

So, avoiding Clayton's gaze and hoping her blush had subsided, she told them how Thomas had spent part of the evening trying to locate the loose wire in the ignition that prevented it from starting. Katie finished her pie and ice cream, stacking her plate.

"That car is begging to be put out of its misery," Max advised.

"I'm going to keep my eye out for a secondhand one we can buy," Lucy said.

Shay set pie before Lucy and in minutes she was enjoying some real home cooking. She'd tried to talk Thomas and Lisa into coming over with her. Thomas would socialize but only when he felt comfortable enough to do it. And Lisa was probably running up the national debt in phone calls keeping in touch with her friends in the city. Suddenly the lights went out, leaving the kitchen in total darkness.

"We've blown a fuse," said Zach. "I'll go fix it."

"Daddy, can we tell scary stories?" Molly asked Josh, her whisper full of excitement at the prospect.

"Not tonight, darlin'."

"I'll get us some light," said Shay. Lucy heard her moving around as Zach left the room. She heard a match strike and then the room was lit by a soft glow. Shay came back to the table carrying two fat wax candles in plastic holders. She placed one at either end of the table then smiled at Lucy. "Eat up. It shouldn't be too long and Zach will have the lights fixed."

Lucy looked back to her plate, cut a sliver of pie and lifted the fork to her mouth. As she did so, she felt a foot nudge her leg under the table. Clayton watched her, a triumphant, oh-so-sexy smile on his face. He raised his mug to her in salute and softly uttered one word.

"Gotcha."

Realization hit her like a ton of bricks. She looked from the candles, to their plates and back to Clayton. He'd won the bet. How could she have let something as innocent as a power failure bring her guard down and not even one week since they'd made the darn wager? Now he would collect his winnings and he wouldn't let her off light, with just a peck on the cheek. Oh, no! He would make certain she was kissed well and truly. Something told her he was good at that, too. And the riding lessons would prove dangerous even if she never fell off the darn horse!

Less than two minutes later the lights came back on and the candles were extinguished, Molly making it a game to see if she could beat her father at blowing them out.

Lucy finished her coffee and pie, trying to ignore the fact that Clayton's feet were nudging hers deliberately, under the table. She pulled them away and cast him an annoyed glare, which only made him grin all the more. After that she didn't dare look at him.

The kids helped Shay to load the dishwasher and Lucy couldn't get them out of there fast enough. She half expected Clayton to follow her out to the car, make some excuse to get her alone, but when they said good-night he merely waved to the kids and told them he would see them in the morning. Then he winked at her, and that one action was filled with intent. It was a warning...a sexy, loaded warning of what was to come and it sent tingles of excitement through her veins.

Clayton McKinley had just put her on notice.

Chapter Four

Lucy would never be sure what woke her later that night, but once she was alert enough to realize something was wrong, she picked up the scent of smoke in the air. Then she identified the strange sound as the horses kicking up a ruckus in their stalls and crying out. She hit the floor running, grabbing her robe from the back of the door on the way past, ramming shoes on her feet. She knew what was wrong before she banged on Thomas's door. He threw it open, already pulling on his shoes, a grim look on his face.

"Fire. The stables, I think. Call the fire brigade!"

Lucy raced downstairs, her heart pounding, adrenaline pumping through her system. When she got outside, the stables were alight but the flames hadn't yet reached the last three stalls where the horses were. The sound of their hooves kicking against the wooden structure frightened her almost as much as the fire.

The smoke threatened to choke her and stung her eyes. She covered her mouth with the hem of her robe and ran to open the stalls. The horses were panicked and Lucy made certain she was out of the way, when one by one she managed to get the stalls open and the horses took off into the night. When she turned around, Thomas was behind her with the garden hose.

The others were outside now, looking at the fire in horror. Lisa retrieved three plastic buckets from the laundry and grabbed a second hose near the shed to fill them. Lucy began dousing what she could of the flames, knowing even as she emptied bucket after bucket onto it, that they would lose the structure, and quite possibly the shed, if the fire got to it.

Lucy saw Katie and Max grab a bucket each but she didn't want them anywhere near the fire. "Start dousing the shed. If we can wet it down we just might save it, but be careful and stay away from the stables." She looked over at Thomas. "Did you call the brigade?"

Thomas nodded, using the hose but hardly making a dent in the blaze that was now roaring as the slight breeze fanned the flames. Lucy wondered if anybody would come to help them. In this country town, as in a lot of others, the bushfire brigade was manned by local volunteers. But ten minutes later the Cable Creek Bushfire Brigade raced down the driveway, another water tanker on the back of a large truck following close behind. Lucy wasn't going to cry. She hadn't cried in years, but her throat tightened as she saw yellow-coated volunteers rushing toward them.

"Lucy!"

She knew that voice. Clayton jumped down from the truck carrying the extra water. Her hands were shaking when he reached her. "Get back. The whole thing could come down on you," he said. Behind him she saw Zach and Josh as well as other men she recognized from businesses in town.

Everyone worked with a common goal, but fate was against them this night as the fire generated its own wind and whipped red-hot cinders under the roof of the shed where it ignited the hay stored for the horses. Fed by dozens of bales, the fire destroyed the structure in less than fifteen minutes and the charred skeleton collapsed in on itself. After that all they could do was douse the smouldering ruins of both buildings. Clayton came up and placed a hand on her shoulder.

"You look like you'll collapse if you don't sit down," he said, leading her to the veranda steps, where she sank to the boards. Lucy felt as if she'd run a marathon. Her legs were shaking and she trembled. "What if I hadn't woken up?" she asked, staring at the smoking rubble. "The fire might have spread to the house."

Thomas stalked across to them, anger radiating from his straight-backed stance. He looked at Clayton. "Did you smell it?"

Clayton nodded after a moment. "Yeah, I did. The brigade captain's going to put in a report to the police."

Lucy listened, their words not making any sense to her. "The police? Why?"

Thomas swore and turned to look back at the ruins. Clayton met her gaze. "Petrol, Lucy. The fire was deliberate."

Katie and Max came up to sit on either side of her, crowding close, their arms around her. Lisa stood near Thomas, her grim expression echoing his rage. Out of instinct she put her arms around the shoulders of her two youngest, but her eyes were fixed on Clayton. "Well, we don't need three guesses as to who's responsible for this, do we?"

Clayton had his suspicions too but he wasn't ready to voice them just yet. Lucy had no such reservations.

"I'll see him in jail for this."

Thomas glared at her. "You know who did this?"

"She doesn't know for sure," said Clayton, hoping to defuse the situation. Finding Gerry and beating him to a pulp wouldn't help the situation, but it would make him feel one hell of a lot better. "The brigade captain will make a report to the police and they'll investigate."

Lucy shook off the hand on her shoulder. "Gerry Anderson wanted this land...you said so yourself, McKinley. And you were the one who told me he wouldn't take humiliation lying down. He told me things happened out here." She shook her head. "We could have all been killed and for what? Because I had to go and tear strips off him in front of his mates. I just didn't think."

Clayton knelt down in front of her and cupped her chin, making her look at him. "This isn't your fault. You were protecting your kids the other night in the pub. The maniac who did this is responsible...not you, Lucy."

His words made sense and his fingers on her skin, stroking, soothing, almost lulled her into believing him...but she couldn't shake the feeling that if she had kept her head and held her tongue, this wouldn't have happened. Since the night of the accident she had kept a tight rein on her emotions. Everything in her life had been carefully planned, methodically controlled.

"Miss Warner?"

She pushed to her feet and met the man who introduced himself as Cappie Gibson, the brigade captain. Lucy also recognized him as the local manager of the hardware store in town. "I'm sorry we couldn't save the stables."

His sincere apology touched her. She ran a shaking hand through her hair. "I understand. You did the best you could. Will you thank your men for me? I appreciate all you did."

He nodded. "Of course." Just then a police car pulled into the yard. "Ah, there's Angus now. I put in a call to him on my mobile phone when we realized the fire was suspicious. Excuse me," he said, walking away toward the police car, stopping for a minute to talk to the officer. When Cappie finally headed toward his men, Angus Willoughby walked up to Lucy.

"Miss Warner. I wish I could say it's nice to see you again...but not under these circumstances."

Despite herself she smiled. Senior Sergeant Angus Willoughby had introduced himself in the grocery store the same week she'd moved here. "It's arson, isn't it?"

"Officially we can't say until the physical-evidence boys get here from Guthrie in the morning," he said, "but unless you're in the habit of splashing a flammable liquid around your stables, then I'd say so. Cappie reported the strong smell of accelerant...petrol. We'll be out here later this morning to scour the remains and gather what we need for our investigation." He took a notebook from inside his jacket and pulled a pen from his pocket. "Now, I just need to ask you a few questions."

Clayton busied himself rolling hoses, but every few seconds his eyes would seek her out. She stood, her arms folded around her waist as though it was the only way she could hold herself together. The pajamas she wore were cotton and no barrier against the cold. The thin material didn't disguise the fact that she wore no bra. Clayton swallowed against the dryness in his throat. The robe she'd pulled on over her nightclothes wasn't much thicker and billowed around her as she walked with Angus. Her hair was down, falling around her shoulders, framing her face, and he was struck with just how hard and fast his attraction to this woman had hit.

Clayton had known desire before and a pretty woman always caught his eye. They were pleasant to be with, soft to touch, warm and willing in his arms. But he couldn't get a handle on this particular woman. He'd felt the attraction to her the minute she'd stormed into the pub, all angry defiance and justified indignation. With other women it had been easy. He would ask them out and they would say yes. Sometimes they asked him first. It was fun. A game. Yet with Lucy the thrill was in the anticipation of not rushing it to completion.

When the call had come in over the two-way radio with the location of the fire, his heart had climbed into his throat and stayed there until they'd pulled up to see her in one piece. That sure as hell had never happened before.

When Angus thanked her and walked toward the burned ruins, Lucy joined the kids, still standing with Zach and Josh. She looked around for Clayton and found him talking to Angus, anger in every line of his body. She was stunned at how much she wanted him to walk toward her, pull her into his arms and just hold her. She couldn't remember ever wanting physical comfort from anyone before. The fact that she wanted it now, from this man, scared her to death.

"How much feed did you lose?" asked Josh, his expression stony.

Lucy dragged her eyes away from Clayton. "It was about half-full. We only had it delivered a week ago."

Josh shoved his hands in the pockets of his moleskins and it was then that Lucy noticed the pager clipped to his belt. It must be a tough grind, she thought, being the only vet in town. "The horses weren't injured?"

"No," she replied. "Scared to death but other than that they seemed okay. The fire hadn't gotten to their stalls by the time I let them out."

Josh took one last look at the ruins. "Well, we've done all we can. If there are still any hot spots among the ashes they won't ignite, not with all that water we poured on there."

The fire truck tooted its horn as it ambled out of the yard, but the McKinleys waited until Angus left. Zach pushed away from the veranda post he'd been leaning against.

"We'd better head home too," he said. "If you want to put the horses up at our place when you catch them, you're more than welcome."

"Thanks. Look, I'm really grateful to you all," she said. "We might have lost the house if you hadn't come."

"We're neighbours," said Zach.

"And friends," Josh added. "You ready, little brother?"

Clayton came up behind her, and when she looked over her shoulder in surprise, he locked his gaze with hers, wanting to soothe her anger and calm her fears. He wanted to say something...anything to make things right. But nothing would make up for what someone had tried to do here tonight. He walked away without a word, and it was the hardest thing he had ever done because everything in him screamed to wrap her in his arms and banish the sadness in her eyes.

Lucy watched the three men walk toward the tanker truck and, close to tears that she refused to let fall, she got the kids inside and up to bed. She hadn't expected him to just turn and walk away, but perhaps it was better this way.

She had no right expecting anything from him. Lucy headed for the bathroom. She showered to get rid of the smoke and ash from her hair and body, standing under the warm stream of water and letting it soothe away the tensions and problems that seemed to surround her.

Megan would never have provoked Gerry. She'd always been calm and logical, the family diplomat. Never once had she failed to intervene on Lucy's behalf with their parents. And in trying to save her little sister's hide yet again, Megan's brilliant future had been snatched away at a city intersection one rainy night.

Lucy had never had much in common with Megan. They'd held different political views, liked music from opposite ends of the spectrum and had different goals in life. But they had been the best of friends. And once she'd lost Megan, Lucy had claimed Megan's dream. Lucy had never allowed anything to sidetrack her in making it a reality.

But now when she looked at Clayton, when he was flirting or being funny and sweet, she felt a hollowness that had never been there before.

She stepped out of the shower stall, drying herself off before dressing in fleecy track pants and a sweatshirt. She spent fifteen minutes blow-drying her hair then she went downstairs, checking the thermostat. Her next stop was the kitchen, where she put coffee on to perk. Lucy heard the vehicle pull into the yard moments later.

Thinking it might be Anderson come to boast about his handiwork...or worse, she went to the front door and looked out the window. The automatic sensor lights had already come on. When she unlocked the door and swung it open, he stood there in the same brown mole-

skin trousers, shirt and boots he'd had on earlier. Now
he had his sheepskin coat on to protect against the chill
and his trousers were smudged here and there with soot.

"McKinley, what are you doing here?"

He opened the screen door and took her hand, pulling
her gently outside. Putting his fingers in his mouth he
gave a low whistle and there came a rustling from the
bushes near the steps. Seconds later a bolt of blue-grey
shot up onto the porch and sat panting obediently at
Clayton's side. It was a heeler of some sort, definitely a
working animal.

"That's a dog."

Clayton grinned. "I knew the wagging tail would give
it away."

She crossed her arms. "Very funny. Now explain to
me what it's doing here." Then she amended her statement. "On second thought, tell me what *you're* doing
here."

"I come bearing gifts," he said easily. "Blue is a
guard dog, one of our best. He'll keep you safe."

He'd gone home to get her a dog because he'd been
worried about her. She would not cry, damn it! How
was he managing to blast through all her defences? He
hadn't made any grand gestures, he hadn't even pres-
sured her since winning the bet. Yet, with this simple
act he brought her close to tears and Lucy never cried.

"You need to go into town sometime and apply for
a firearms license," he said, his tone brooking no ar-
gument. "Then we'll get you a rifle."

Lucy stiffened. "I don't like guns," she said firmly.

Clayton tempered his impatience and knew to take his
time. "Used properly and kept out of the wrong hands,
a gun is useful on a property. And if Anderson or anyone
else comes here with the intention of doing you or the

kids harm, you let him see the rifle. If he doesn't take the hint, aim into the air and let off a shot to let him know you're not afraid to use it.''

Lucy hated weapons and always had. ''I moved out here to get my kids away from violence and you want me to bring a weapon into the house?''

He took two steps and closed the distance between them. He was so close beneath the bright porch light she could see the pale grey flecks in his blue eyes. He reached out and cupped her chin in his hand, the touch of skin on skin mesmerizing.

''What I want is for you to be safe. To be able to protect yourself. Every home around here has at least one gun.''

She scowled and he let his hand drop to his side. ''That doesn't make them a good idea.''

''More a necessary evil, I'd say. Humour me, okay?''

Lucy would need time to think about it. ''I'm so angry with Anderson right now, if I were the violent type I'd—''

''You'd stay away from him, Lucy, even if I had to tie you up. He means business.''

Lucy had an overdeveloped streak of suspicion. Anyone who worked with kids had it. It was working now. ''You know something, don't you?'' He glanced away, breaking eye contact with her for a split second, but that was all she needed. ''Tell me, McKinley. After the night I've had I deserve the truth.''

He didn't speak for a moment then he shoved his hands into the pockets of his jacket. ''One of the guys in the brigade is also the bartender at the Roadhouse. According to him, Gerry was there mouthing off the other night.''

Lucy steeled herself. ''And?''

"He joked that maybe he should just torch the place, burn it to the ground. He said then you'd get the message that you weren't wanted here."

She gaped. "Did anyone tell the police?"

"I don't think so. Nobody took him seriously. But Angus knows now. He'll take it from here."

Lucy swore and he reached for her, but she pulled away. "I need to be angry for a minute or two, and I can't get it out of my system with you touching me." She crossed her arms in front of her and shook her head. "You know the funniest thing about all this?" she asked. "We're not renting from Gray. He's letting us live here as caretakers. He only makes a profit when we can get this place functioning as a working farm again." She looked at him with tired eyes. "Gerry doesn't stand a chance of getting this place even if we did leave, doesn't he understand that?"

Clayton rubbed the back of his neck. "I don't think it's to do with you being here so much now," he said, hating like hell to say it. "This is revenge, Lucy."

She'd known it deep down, but to hear him say it chilled her. Gerry could have killed Max if the horse had thrown him into the path of the car or if the animal had stepped on the boy. Tonight their house could have burned to the ground with one good gust of wind, while they slept inside.

"I'll think about getting a gun."

Clayton didn't betray how pleased he was. He schooled his features to an impassive mask. The wary eyes, the deep frown and grim set lips told him how much it was costing her to give the idea consideration. She even managed a smile as she reached out to the dog, who sniffed her hand and then licked her fingers. "He likes me."

Clayton liked the way she was taking to the animal, petting it and letting it nuzzle and lick her hand. He sighed heavily, wondering how the hell a man could be jealous of a dog. She looked up, smiling at him in a way that had him wanting to haul her off to the nearest bed and keep her there.

"Well," she said, "I'd better let you get home. Thanks for Blue."

"I'm not going home."

"Well, you're not staying here!"

He nodded. "Yes I am. Right here until daybreak. On the veranda swing."

She barely resisted the urge to stamp her foot. "This is ridiculous. You can't camp out on my doorstep. Apart from the fact that you'll freeze, what will people think?"

He shrugged, shoving his hands into the pockets of his trousers. "It's warmer tonight than it has been lately."

Lucy scoffed. "If you're a polar bear, maybe."

"And I don't really give a flying fig what anyone thinks about what I choose to do. Besides, who's going to know except you and me?" he asked, ignoring her remark.

"I can take care of myself. I've got a dog now."

"Don't forget those self-defence lessons you took a few years back."

So he thought she was harmless? Well, some day she might just have to show him how much attention she had paid to those lessons. "Look, the fire shook me up, okay?" she said, willing to admit that much. "But you'll be a wreck come morning if you don't get some rest."

"I'll bum a blanket off you," he said, walking to the swing and settling himself in it. "Right here will be fine."

She made a sound of pure frustration. "God save me from stubborn men," she said, looking toward the heavens.

Clayton watched her walk inside, thankful that at least now she might manage to get some sleep without worrying about her family's safety. She was angry with him but it wouldn't last forever. And it didn't really matter. His own gut instinct told him Gerry had been behind the fire tonight. He shifted on the swing, admitting that the couch inside would have been more comfortable. But that was the problem. It would be too comfortable and she would be too close.

Day by day the attraction got stronger, more intense and far more physical. All set to endure the night imagining her upstairs, stretched out in her bed, he was surprised when the door opened ten minutes later and Lucy came out, a large, thick quilt in one hand, a mug of coffee in the other. She dropped the quilt in his lap.

"I thought about using it to muffle the screams when I murdered you, but I'm too exhausted to bother."

He spread out the blanket and took the mug from her. "You should get to bed," he told her, making himself comfortable as the dog curled up at his feet.

"I won't sleep," she replied, needing so badly to get off her feet, to wind down. She sat down beside him, realizing just how small the swing really was when she found herself pressed against his side. She stilled for a few seconds and when he made no comment, she started the swing rocking slightly with her foot.

"Well, if you're going to sit out here, you're sure as hell not going to get a chill," he said, handing her his mug while he pulled the quilt over them, tucking it around her. The heavy stuffing would work with their own body heat to keep them warm. He took his mug back from her and settled into a cosy position, their thighs touching, her body stiff and unyielding.

"How did you do it?"

"Do what?"

"Get the lights to go out tonight so Shay would have to use candles. Did you pay one of the hands to stand by the fuse box and wait for some kind of signal?"

Clayton chuckled and reached his arm around her shoulder, the action leaning her farther into him, while his fingers began stroking the top of her shoulder, bared by the large neckline of the sweatshirt. He knew she hadn't bothered putting on a bra beneath it, felt the side of one full, soft breast pressing into his chest. *God, the army could use this as a form of torture.*

Lucy tried to concentrate on anything but his fingers, now drawing invisible patterns on her soft skin. "So you're telling me it was…what? Accident? Fate? Hand of God?"

He smiled. "We have trouble with the wiring sometimes. It's an old house."

Lucy accepted the explanation…until she could prove otherwise. "You don't have to keep stroking my shoulder, you know."

He leaned his head close to hers, his lips a whisper away from her ear. "Yes, I do, Lucy. It's either stroke your shoulder or kiss you senseless."

Lucy caught her breath at the husky intent in his tone. "Well, you did win the bet," she said tightly, trying not to notice how his warm breath tickled the shell of her ear. "I do owe you."

She certainly did and Clayton couldn't remember a time when he'd delayed. The meeting, the attraction, the kiss…all eventually leading to a mutually satisfying relationship. Lucy was different. His attraction to her was more intense. He was finding it much more satisfying by prolonging that first physical intimacy between them. Kissing a woman before had never been as special as it would be with Lucy.

"You sound as enthusiastic as someone about to be led to the gallows."

She glanced up at him and then looked away. "At least that would be quick."

"But not nearly as much fun."

Lucy scowled and looked up at him. "Can we just get it over and done with? You're driving me to distraction with your fingers."

"Oh, darlin'," he said, catching her chin so she couldn't look away. "Some day I'll show you just how distracting my fingers can be when they have a mind to."

"Well...if you don't want to kiss me then that's fine," she said, her tone curt.

Clayton threw his head back and laughed. Lucy felt the vibrations all through her body. "It really is annoying you that finally there's something out of your control, something you have no say in."

The frown deepened. His words came a little too close to the truth. "Are you saying I'm a control freak, McKinley?"

He stopped chuckling and became serious. "I think you like to know how life is going to go, Lucy. I'll bet you plan ahead, never leave anything to chance and always look twice before you leap."

If I'm so clearheaded why aren't I running from you?

"We're both exhausted, Lucy. The kiss will keep, trust me, and by the time I get around to it you might be ready to admit that you like me."

She wasn't at all comfortable with the way they were

sitting, her body plastered to his from chest to thigh, but pushing away would mean touching him and she figured sitting here was the lesser of two very dangerous evils.

"I never said I didn't like you. I said I wasn't getting involved with you."

"You'll change your mind."

"You want to bet on it?" she asked, remembering too late the mess she was in from the last bet they made. "On second thought, forget that."

The sensor lights timed off, leaving them with the moonlight as their chaperon and a sky full of stars to dazzle them.

"How are the kids working out?" she asked him.

"They're enthusiastic. They do every task I set them and still come back for more, but there is one thing," he said, not quite sure how to broach the subject. "Max…told me about his mother." When Lucy looked up in surprise, he nodded. "Yeah, kind of caught me off guard too."

Lucy had seen the way the boy looked at Clayton. He trusted him. "The only other person I know he's told is Thomas."

He shook his head, still amazed at how calmly Max had talked about it. "He asked me about my parents. I told him my mum died when I was young, just a little younger than he is now. But it's hard trying to forget the image he painted for me."

Lucy knew what was going through his mind. She would have seen it in his eyes even if she hadn't heard it in his voice. "Don't think about it too much," she warned. "You'll go crazy trying to figure out why people do the things they do."

"She beat him so badly he had to be hospitalized, Lucy." The disbelief in his voice momentarily drowned out the anger. "How could someone do that to their own child?"

Chapter Five

"I could tell you stories that would make it sound like Max got off lightly. It's true," she said when he looked at her. "His mother hurt him so badly no judge in his right mind would ever give him back to her...even if she weren't in jail. Max is one of the lucky ones."

His jaw clenched. "I'm sure he felt really lucky."

She sighed, looking up at the stars. "Thomas worked a miracle with him. He took Max under his wing, included him in everything he did, told him stories and taught him some boxing moves." She smiled. "He made a huge difference."

"I don't think he likes me."

"Max? Of course he does."

"Thomas," he corrected. "He's suspicious of me."

"Thomas is suspicious of everyone, McKinley, so don't take it personally."

"He trusts you."

"I've known him since he was twelve. He was the hardest to reach of all the kids. He hated me at first...but most of all he hated himself.'' She sighed heavily. ''I'm grateful for the fact that he's come so far.''

Clayton guessed she was downplaying her role in helping both boys. He could imagine that she fought for them with all her might, with as much courage as she had shown that night at the pub. He had come to know them pretty well. Katie was fourteen going on forty. Thomas looked at the world through weary nineteen-year-old eyes that had seen too much. Lisa was two years younger and rebellious.

''Do all the kids come from abusive backgrounds?''

''Yes, either physical, mental, sexual, though it's more often than not a combination of at least two.''

''I feel almost guilty for the childhood I had,'' he said. ''Growing up, I thought every kid had trees to climb, creeks to swim in and parents who would die to keep them safe.'' Clayton cursed into the night. ''These kids…''

Lucy liked the way the moonlight glinted off his hair. ''They survived, McKinley.'' His jaw was clenched, his mouth a grim line. Even his fingers had stilled on her neck and shoulder. ''You know, breaking my coffee mug isn't going to get you a return invitation.''

Clayton loosened his grip on the mug. Their eyes met and held. ''I don't believe I've ever been invited,'' he told her, a wry smile on his lips. ''The first time I invited myself and this time I refused to go home.''

She yawned, fighting exhaustion. ''Pushy must be genetic with you as well.''

He chuckled. ''You've been talking to Shay.''

They fell into a comfortable silence there in the moon-lit hours of morning, the swing rocking gently, Clayton with his arm around Lucy.

''So, when can I expect you for your riding lesson?''

Lucy shook her head. "McKinley, teaching me to ride a horse will be like teaching the horse to roller-skate. It would be a waste of your time and mine."

"I disagree."

She chuckled. "Why am I not surprised?"

"I'm serious. We can ride together until you feel confident enough to go by yourself."

Lucy smiled. "Together meaning on the same horse."

"Why not?"

How many reasons did the man want? "I'll trade you two kisses for no riding lessons."

He shrugged. "No deal. When I kiss you I intend to do it more than once," he promised her. "Besides, lessons will come in handy when you get this place up and running productively again. Checking fences is always a lot more fun on horseback."

Lucy sighed, irritation warring with anticipation. "Does the word *no* mean anything to you?"

"Sure. I just don't hear it that often."

She couldn't help the chuckle that bubbled up from inside her. "Oh, all right! You can give me one lesson. One." His sigh was pure contentment and she couldn't find it in her to be annoyed with him.

"Try to get some sleep."

Sitting practically in his lap? With his arm around her and the warmth of his body seeping into hers? And after the conversation they'd just had? Sleep was the last thing on her mind even though she felt exhausted. In the last ten minutes she had told Clayton more about her chosen family than she'd ever told anyone. Company was something she hadn't missed before, intimacy something she hadn't craved...until Clayton.

She'd known from that first night by the side of the road that he was dangerous. Even with Shay's words about him being determined when he wanted something echoing in her head, the danger coaxed her closer. She closed her eyes, determined not to doze off, but the strong beating of his heart and the slow rocking motion of the swing combined to soothe her body and her mind.

Clayton knew the moment when she finally succumbed to fatigue. He kept the swing rocking gently, listening to her deep, even breathing. He reached out, stroking errant strands of hair off her face, gently, so as not to wake her. It felt right having her curl up against him under the heavy quilt. When he was with her, even just talking to her or watching her, he felt pulled under her spell.

Asleep she seemed vulnerable, something most people would probably never equate with the Lucy Warner he had met on Saturday night. She seemed fragile.

After twenty minutes he couldn't feel his arm and shifted slightly to get sensation back into the limb. Lucy raised her head but didn't open her eyes. He pulled her head softly to his shoulder and she stilled once more. He leaned his head against hers, tempted to give in to the exhaustion clawing at him but far too keyed up to think about sleep. He was caught up in the enigma of Lucy.

She was a complicated woman with secrets, and yet her life, her attitude to it, seemed so simple. He'd bet the farm that people around her usually knew when to back away, especially when she drew that prickly shell around herself. He had no doubt that half the time it actually worked. He had seen the first cracks in the armour though. The way she joked with him. The trust she gave him by sleeping in his arms. It was enough for now.

Dawn was splashing the sky with brilliant colours of mauve and orange, pink and red when she stirred again.

"Hey, sleepyhead."

Lucy shivered slightly though it was toasty warm beneath the quilt. Her dream was too good to leave, too enticing to end...but she knew it had to. Another day, more work to do. She stifled a yawn and opened her eyes to find herself caught in the pure blue gaze of eyes that watched her intently. McKinley! It hadn't been a dream. When Lucy realized she was more or less lying on top of him, she pushed at his chest and moved away.

Clayton gave her a wry look. "I don't bite...unless I'm asked."

"I believe that," she said, taking a deep breath of chilled misty morning air. It seared her lungs and woke up every part of her body but it was the quickest way to clear her head of him. The sun was rising in earnest now, rising majestically over the horizon. "I should wake Katie just to prove to her the sun really does rise this early."

She looked up at him. "Since you watched over us last night I'm offering you breakfast."

Clayton sat up and stretched. He ran a hand over his face and nodded. "Best invitation I've had in weeks."

Lucy reached up to brush the hair from her eyes. He had to be sore from sitting on the swing all night. She could feel the ache in her muscles already and groaned as she straightened her spine.

"I take it you aren't a morning person," he commented while watching her move.

"I'm with Katie on this one. I like morning just fine as long as it starts a little later in the day." She looked at the sunrise. "Isn't it beautiful? It's as if God is painting something wonderful to make up for all the ugliness in the world."

Clayton had seen a lot of sunrises and had begun to

take them for granted. To him the sunrise had always meant the start of another day, more work to be done. This sunrise, his first with Lucy, was one he would always remember.

"Geez, man, you must want to impress the hell out of Lucy."

Thomas stood in the doorway shaking his head, and Clayton found himself grinning back. He'd been sitting here drinking coffee for the last twenty minutes, wondering about Lucy and contemplating those riding lessons. The young man was dressed in jeans, sneakers and a shirt. He looked at the mug Clayton held. He shook his head and walked to the fridge. "Nobody drinks her coffee voluntarily."

Clayton couldn't very well argue with him. "It's starting to grow on me."

Thomas poured himself a glass of juice. "Yeah, like something mean and nasty," he said, coming to sit at the table. "You know, you're the only person I know who can get Lucy to do things she wouldn't normally do."

"Anything specific?"

"She told me she's thinking of getting a rifle. Since I know she hates guns, I'm thinking you had something to do with persuading her."

Clayton wasn't going to start backing off from the truth with Thomas. "I asked her to think about it. That doesn't mean she'll actually go ahead and get one."

Thomas shrugged and took a sip of juice. "You stayed last night. I heard the vehicle come back and saw your truck out my window. After a while I got up to check she was okay."

"I won't hurt her, Thomas…and I won't let anyone else hurt her either."

Thomas smiled coolly, seeming far too wise for his tender years. "You'd better not hurt her, McKinley, because you'll never get another chance with her if you do. She'll make sure of it."

When Lucy came into the kitchen, dressed in jeans, sneakers and a sweatshirt, Thomas fell silent. She looked uncertainly from one to the other, pouring herself coffee and setting the table with cereal, bowls, milk and juice.

Thomas cleared his throat. "We can't touch that mess out there until the cop comes back. What do you want me to do today?"

"We've got to find the horses and make sure they're not hurt."

Thomas gave a slight smile. "They were waiting when I went outside this morning. It didn't take much to coax them to me. I tied them up and gave them some water."

"I'll tether them to the back of my truck and take them home with me when I go," said Clayton before sipping his coffee. "I'll give them a feed and get Josh to take a look to make sure they weren't injured."

Thomas finished his juice and stood. "I'd better keep going on the scraping."

When the boy was gone Lucy studied Clayton. "You should go home and get some sleep."

He stifled a yawn and shook his head. "Katie and I have a water pump to fix over at the Downs."

"I'll find plenty here today to keep them busy. Once Angus and his men are finished sifting through what used to be my stables, we'll get busy clearing it up. The water pump isn't going anywhere."

Clayton nodded. "I'll do it if you'll set aside an hour this afternoon and come over to the Downs."

Lucy frowned. "Why?"

"Surprise," he said, ending the conversation as the kids descended on the kitchen.

Lucy was ambushed that afternoon. Clayton was leading a horse from the stables when she pulled up. She got out of her car and walked toward him.

"Did Josh take a look at the horses?"

He nodded. "They're fine. Has Angus been and gone?"

Lucy used her hand to shield her eyes from the sun. "Yeah. He thinks he got what he needed."

Clayton's jaw clenched. "Good," he said sharply, then he smiled. "Ready for your lesson?"

"I don't have time right now, McKinley."

He merely smiled, using his hat to knock the dust off his moleskin trousers. "A riding lesson or the kiss, Lucy. Your choice."

Lucy scowled. "Isn't that a bit like asking the condemned man whether he wants to be hanged or shot?"

He chuckled, shaking his head. "Neither of your choices is life-threatening."

She glanced at the horse, feeling the urge to move away from the big animal. "Don't bet on it."

"Come on, Birdie's the gentlest horse we've got," he said, smoothing his hand up between her eyes and down over her nose. The animal responded, nuzzling his hand. For one insane moment Lucy wished she were the horse, his hands stroking over her so expertly. She took a deep breath and kept her eyes focused on the horse. *Why did these feelings have to surface now?*

For as long as she could remember she'd been able to

distance herself, shut down her emotions and give of herself only what she felt comfortable with. Yet every time she was around Clayton she felt new and exciting things, emotions her body welcomed, as if it knew them, craved them. Her fingers itched to reach out and touch him, to smooth over hard muscle and bronzed skin. She wanted to touch and be touched in return.

"I love seeing you blush, Lucy, but I like it even better when I know why you're blushing," he said, his expression questioning.

"There are some things you're better off not knowing, McKinley," she said, daring him to challenge her. When he didn't, she straightened her shoulders. "So, what do I do first?"

Clayton walked to the nearby fence and lifted the saddle into his arms, smiling to himself. He'd had a lot of women look at him, assess him as a man. But no woman had ever surveyed him with the intensity Lucy just had. He'd felt the caress of her eyes as though she were touching him with those delicate fingers of hers. And that was just what he wanted. Lucy in his arms. In his bed. The two of them and nothing but time to explore each other.

Clayton turned back to find her reaching out a tentative hand to Birdie. She faced her fears. When running from them would have been easier, Lucy stood her ground, and that strength drew him to her. He'd desired women before but never with the compelling, gut-twisting need that Lucy fueled in him. Dressed as she was this morning in the obligatory jeans and shirt, her hair in that ponytail she was so fond of, Lucy looked sexy and very touchable.

Fifteen minutes later Clayton had saddled the horse and Lucy felt a little easier about riding her. Nerves formed a knot in her stomach as Clayton explained where her hand and foot went on the saddle. He did it once to show her how and Lucy caught her breath at the fluid motion. He used the total synchronicity of every muscle and sinew in his body. He sat tall in the saddle, with an air of confidence Lucy was beginning to warm to in him. He reached a hand down to her.

"I really think I should ride by myself."

He shook his head. "Not the first time. Climb up here with me and Birdie will take us for a walk. You two girls can get acquainted."

Lucy looked at the small space between the V of his thighs and the pommel, knowing if she accepted his offer she'd know him a whole lot more intimately than she did now.

"There's not much room up there. I don't want you to be uncomfortable," she said, cringing at how lame her excuse sounded. His sexy smile melted her.

"Darlin', if there was a mile between me and that pommel I'd be uncomfortable with your cute little backside nestled between my legs," he said, his eyes a deeper blue than she had seen before. "But I can control myself," he said dryly, "even if I can't control my body's response to you. So let me lift you up here and we can get going."

His honesty would get him in trouble someday, she knew. *He was going to be uncomfortable? How did he think she was going to feel?* She was celibate, not stupid. The two of them together on that saddle, their bodies moving against each other and the desire simmering in his eyes...it was a dangerous combination.

Lucy had learned—the hard way—the value of thinking before acting. Look before you leap could have been invented with her in mind, but the more she thought about getting up on that horse and sitting her backside between his legs, the less sure she felt about it.

"I'm not exactly a lightweight."

But as if she hadn't spoken, he leaned over and placed his hands at her waist and lifted her as though she weighed nothing. Her fingers dug into his forearms and she felt the muscle flex beneath them.

When he had her settled in her place, he scooted his backside just a little farther back. Before Lucy could breathe a sigh of relief that he was going to make this as easy as possible for her, he placed a hand to her stomach and moved her back a scant inch until she felt him against her.

Lucy sat rigid trying to ignore that he was halfway aroused. "McKinley, this really isn't a good idea."

His arms came around her and gave her a sense of security. When he leaned close enough that she could feel his warm breath in her ear, she shivered.

"Begging your pardon, Lucy, but I think it's a damn good idea. Now, if you'll just relax your body back into mine and trust me not to let you fall, you might just enjoy this."

He sure as hell intended to. Her nerves made him smile. He found the slight trembling of her body endearing. But it was her curvaceous backside that he was most aware of, pressed intimately against him, just as he had expected.

Birdie had been walking for a full minute before Lucy relaxed against him, little by little, almost testing the waters. He guided the horse down the trail that led away from the homestead, away from where the others were working this morning and down toward the creek that cut through their southernmost paddock.

"Where are you taking me?"

"You say that like you don't trust me, Lucy."

She shifted her hip slightly and felt his arousal more sharply than before. When Clayton sucked in his breath, she froze. "I'm sorry."

"We're adults, Lucy," he said, breathing deeply. "Not two high-school kids who don't know what happens when two people are attracted to each other and put in this position."

"You put us in this position," she reminded him, annoyance in her tone.

Clayton smiled. At least she hadn't denied she was attracted to him. That was progress. "I was thinking of your safety, Lucy."

"Are you sure you're not Irish?"

He shook his head. "Scottish. Why?"

"Because I've never heard anyone with such a gift for the blarney," she replied.

He relished her sigh as she spotted the creek. He wondered if she saw the beauty as he did. The trees, the profusion of wildflowers and the majestic blue hills in the distance.

The ride down here had taken them no more than ten minutes, but in that time his arousal had passed mild and was headed toward highly pleasurable. He almost groaned aloud at the thought of losing that intimate contact with her, but then he thought about the ride home and smiled to himself.

"This is it," he said, pulling on the reins to halt Birdie. He was no sooner on the ground than he watched as Lucy bit on her bottom lip for a few seconds, then grasped the pommel and swung her leg over the horse.

When she stood beside him, the smile on her face at that accomplishment warmed him like sunshine. Such a small thing, something he never thought about, yet to

Lucy it was a new skill, something she'd learned even through her fear.

"My legs feel a little funny."

"It's from gripping the horse between your thighs," he told her, trying not to imagine those thighs in too much detail. "Give it a few minutes."

She nodded, walking slowly, testing each leg as she went down toward the creek. "It's beautiful here," she said, hands in the back pockets of her jeans. "Is this the creek that runs through my place?"

"Yeah," he said, coming up beside her.

"How did the town come to be named after it?" she asked, leaning down to pick a jonquil.

"Jonathon Cable came here during the gold rush of the 1800s," he said. "Everyone told him he was wasting his time, that this place had been mined dry, but he wasn't easily dissuaded. When he did strike gold, he bought this parcel of land and eventually everything around it that is Cable Downs. Then he named the town and the creek after himself and decreed that the property always be run by his family."

Lucy looked up at him, surprised. "So you're his descendant?"

Clayton nodded. "He was my great-great-grandfather. He married a girl who had come this way to be a housemaid to a wealthy couple, took her out of her life of service and built her a beautifully ornate home here on the Downs." He interpreted her questioning look. "It burned to the ground during a bushfire twenty years later."

Lucy looked around her, marveling at how Jonathon might have stood on this very spot, imagining the house he would build for his love, the property he would nurture, one that still thrived today. "But your name isn't Cable."

He grinned. "Thank the Lord for small favours," he said, then looking heavenward, he added, "No offence there, Jonathon." He looked back to her. "My mother was an only child. She met Dad on a trip to the city. He was rodeoing at the time, but one look at her and he gave it up to come back here and be a farmer. When my grandfather died, my father took over the running of the Downs."

"Did you ever think of leaving here? Maybe to travel or do something else besides farming?"

Clayton sat down on the grass, patting the ground beside him until Lucy dropped down also. "I rodeoed for a few years in my early twenties, but I always came back home. The last time was for good."

Lucy sighed and twirled the wildflower between her fingers. "I went to a rodeo once when I was young," she said, smiling at him. "I barracked for the bull...or the horse, whatever the ringers were trying to ride." He chuckled and shook his head casting her a dry look. "Well, it can't be much fun for the animals and only an insane person would climb on something big and mean enough to kill him, just to prove it can be ridden."

"What does that make my three years on the circuit?"

She smiled. "A momentary lapse in good judgement. Besides, I'll bet all those women you've dated have been pleased all your parts are still in working order."

He chuckled and shook his head. "Curious?"

"About the women you've dated?"

He grinned wickedly. "About all my parts being in working order."

Lucy threw her head back and laughed. "I'll live with the suspense."

They were quiet for the next few minutes, each lost in their own thoughts. Finally Clayton took her hand and aligned their palms, fingers entwining. "Why are you afraid of getting involved with me, Lucy? Do you think I'll break your heart?"

Lucy chewed her bottom lip, her eyes on him. "My heart's pretty well insulated." She'd lived with her parents' pain and resentment after the accident. Her heart had become scarred over. "What do you want, McKinley?"

He grinned broadly. "You."

"In other words, sex."

Clayton raised an eyebrow, but his eyes remained focused on her. "Eventually. *I want you.* I want you to get sassy with me and give me a hard time. I want to slow dance with you to some soppy country song and I want to know what it feels like when you go all soft and warm in my arms."

Lucy couldn't look away from him, her heart pounding at the image he'd painted for her. "McKinley, my life up to this point has consisted of school, university and my career…in that order. I've never had time for an affair."

Clayton couldn't remember a time when he had wanted a woman more. If they had an affair, it wouldn't be a flash in the pan. He would want her over and over again. Once with her in his arms, in his bed, would never be enough. "Then it's time you made space in your life for a man. Me."

Lucy couldn't help a smile. Did nothing catch this man off guard? she wondered. "I know from experience that arguing with you would be a waste of time and energy."

"Does that mean you're going to become putty in my

hands and give yourself up to my most secret desires and fantasies?'' he asked, his eyebrows waggling wickedly.

Lucy doubted she would even survive the experience he described. ''Putty? I don't think so.'' Then she smiled at him. ''The desires and fantasies might be negotiable.''

''I drive a hard bargain,'' he warned her, a glint in his eye.

''I'll bet.'' She pushed herself to stand, brushing off her jeans. They had come a long way on this short ride to the creek, farther than she had ever expected to go with this man. ''I really should get back, McKinley.''

Clayton nodded, standing to lead the way back up the creek bank to where Birdie was tethered.

On the ride back, he held her as snugly as the first time, their bodies moving with the motion of the horse, rubbing against each other intimately, but neither said a word.

The idea of an affair with him was tempting. The moment she'd let him into her house that first night, he had seeped into her life despite her best efforts to keep him out. Now she wanted him against her best intentions.

Chapter Six

"You've got it bad for Lucy, haven't you?"

Clayton smiled at the understatement and tried not to get his fingers caught between two cogs. He'd been working on the water pump for two hours and trying to concentrate on it rather than on his ride with Lucy yesterday. Until now he'd been succeeding and Katie had been content with asking questions about everything he did and handing him the tools he asked for.

Clayton wiped his forehead with the back of his head. "I like her," he admitted. "She's a good person."

Katie rolled her eyes. "I'm not ten years old, Clayton. I know what gets a man interested in a woman."

Amused at her world-weary sigh, he raised an eyebrow. "Really? Do tell."

She perched on the hood of his Jeep, brushing dust from her jeans. "Well, it's obvious. She's pretty and she's got a nice body. Trust me, guys never look any further than the obvious."

He thought about her words for a moment, idly fingering the spanner in his hand. "That's an awfully cynical attitude for someone your age."

She shrugged carelessly. "It's true."

"Well, I'll let you in on a little secret," he said, laying the spanner down to wipe his hands on the greasy rag he pulled from his back pocket. "I like Lucy for who she is."

"And if she looked like one of those old witches out of the storybooks?"

Clayton laughed, unable to picture Lucy any other way than how she was. "I'd still like her, wart and all."

Katie gave him a mocking grin. "But it doesn't hurt that she's beautiful, does it?"

"No, it doesn't, but there's part of her that's beautiful in a way that isn't easily seen."

Katie nodded shrewdly. "You know she thinks you're stubborn."

Clayton grinned, arching his back against the strain of leaning over the pump. "She's right."

"Lucy says you could teach obstinacy to mules."

"Yeah, well, I think it's a trait we have in common."

Katie bit her bottom lip. "You won't hurt her."

"No, Katie, I won't."

"Good, because if you did, I'd have to hurt you," she told him, half-serious. "Then I'd get Thomas to hurt you some more."

Clayton nodded. "I'll keep that in mind."

"She's a special person."

The love in Katie's voice wasn't a surprise to him. "She means a lot to you, that's plain to see."

"I remember the last foster home I was in," she said, raising her eyes to him. "They sent me back to the state home. Said I wasn't what they were looking for. I mean, I talk too much sometimes and back then I was kind of clumsy." She shrugged. "They were the ninth couple to send me back."

Clayton swallowed the giant-size lump in his throat. He reached up and tugged on one of her braids. "They were all fools who didn't know what a gem they had."

Katie beamed. "Thanks. But it was okay, in fact going back to the home was the best thing that could have happened to me because that same week Lucy came to see the administrator about something...and I'd just flooded the bathroom by accident."

Clayton was amazed that this girl could laugh about such a traumatic time in her life. Would anyone ever know the battering her self-esteem had taken at being rejected so many times? "Lucy rescued you?"

Katie grinned and nodded. "Water was flowing like a flooded river had burst its banks and the administrator was yelling. She threw her arms up and went so red in the face I thought she'd have a fit!" She chuckled and Clayton found himself smiling with her. "She told me no one in their right mind would ever want me as part of their family."

Clayton didn't need to be told what effect that would have had on Lucy. He'd seen her motherly instincts in full flight. "She was wrong."

"That's what Lucy said...only not in those words," she said, leaving him in no doubt as to how she'd said it. "The next thing I knew I was living with Lucy in the house she rented. I went to school and made friends. Then she got the okay for this project, and though I wasn't a street kid I still got to come out here."

Clayton knew that nothing this side of hell would have stopped Lucy from bringing Katie with her to Cable Creek. Did the woman even realize what a difference she had made to the lives of the kids she had helped?

"So, is it fixed?" she asked, pointing to the pump.

Clayton shoved the rag back in his pocket. "I sure hope so. I can think of things I'd rather be doing." He began to gather up the tools.

"Clayton, would you help me do something nice for Lucy? You know, to kind of make up for the fire and everything?"

He walked to the truck and deposited the tools into the back. "Sure. What did you have in mind?"

She shrugged and smiled at him. "Depends how many nice people you know and how persuasive you can be."

Lucy was lying in bed early on Saturday morning, contemplating the kiss she owed Clayton when she heard the unmistakable sound of vehicles, not one but many, pulling into the yard. At the same moment, Katie poked her head around the door.

"You'd better get dressed, Lucy. They're here already."

"Who's here?"

Katie smiled. "It's a surprise. Hurry up," she said, closing the door as she left. Lucy rushed out of bed and raced to the window. She counted ten cars, six four-wheel drives and two flatbed trucks. People piled out of every door. One of the trucks carried timber, the other corrugated roofing iron.

None of this made sense. These people were from town, she knew, recognizing some of the faces. What on earth were they doing here? Then she spotted Clayton, talking and laughing as he joined both his brothers in unloading the timber.

Lucy searched for clothes, her mind on one thing only...the activity in her yard. She dressed in jeans, a white singlet top and good sturdy boots.

She brushed her hair and pulled it into a ponytail before heading downstairs. Her kitchen was a hive of activity, and of all the women milling around, the one she was most relieved to see was Shay.

"You don't mind us putting all this stuff in here, do you?"

"All this stuff" consisted of salads, rice dishes, hot pots, baked whole potatoes and at least five desserts that looked sinfully good. All manner of meat cuts lay on trays covered with plastic wrap. Lamb chops, thick steaks and sausages, enough to feed a small army...like the one massing in her yard.

"Of course you can," she replied. "But what's going on? Why is everybody here?"

Shay smiled. "I believe Clayton was hoping to do the honours. But I'll introduce you to the other ladies before we head out."

Lucy spent the next ten minutes chatting to the women, only a handful of whom she knew. Constance Willoughby was a local schoolteacher and seemed pleased that Max and Katie were enrolled to start the new term on Monday. Lucy was surprised that she and Angus were not twins, so alike were their looks.

She greeted Dulcie Jenkins, owner of the general store, and met her granddaughter, Justine, Cable Creek's only photographer.

Lucy smiled politely and shook hands with each newly introduced person, but she itched to know what was going on, and by the time Shay finally led her outside, her curiosity was killing her.

Shay called out to Clayton and beckoned him over then excused herself to go back inside.

Dressed in jeans, boots and a cotton work shirt the

same blue as his eyes, he shouldn't have sent her pulse into overdrive.

She'd seen him dressed this way before. But one smile set her heart racing and she couldn't remember what her life had been like without him in it. There had been times in the past week when she'd lain in her bed, imagining how his callused fingers would glide across her flesh, how soft his lips would be on her body.

She'd never been one to fantasize, at least not about sex, but Clayton set her mind to wandering into all kinds of dangerous territory. Lucy dragged her mind back from wicked thoughts. "You did all this?"

He shrugged, tucking work gloves into the back pocket of his jeans. "It was Katie's idea. All I did was make a few phone calls."

"A few phone calls? Half the town must be here."

"Not quite," he said, taking her hand in his as he pulled her toward the house.

"McKinley, what on earth—"

"I wouldn't make a scene," he said, turning a brief but melting smile on her. "Not unless you want an audience."

An audience for what? And where the hell was he taking her like some overbearing Neanderthal. He took off his hat as they entered the house. In the kitchen most of the women were still there. "Ladies." Lucy counted more than a few speculative glances and one wry grin from Shay at Clayton's polite address.

He led her down the hall and into the laundry. As the door whispered closed behind them she whirled on him, her questions forgotten as he looked at her with pure desire. "God knows what those women are thinking," she said, wiping suddenly sweaty palms down her jeans.

"Letting them form their own opinions about what's going on is probably better than the truth."

"What truth?" she asked, exasperated. "I don't even know what's going on."

He threw his hat and it sailed through the air, landing neatly on a basket of clean towels. He took a step toward her, stopping with barely an inch separating them.

"I'm collecting on the other part of our bet," he said, his voice more seductive than she'd ever heard it. "It's time to pay up, Lucy."

The kiss! He wanted to kiss her now? Lucy's body hummed with excitement. "I still think you cheated."

His smile was a wicked challenge. "You can't prove it."

"Then kiss me and get it over with."

He chuckled. "I suppose a little enthusiasm would be out of the question?"

Lucy bit back a smile. "I've been kissed before, McKinley."

"Not by me."

Clayton hadn't planned on kissing her right now, but if he was going to get anything done today he'd at least do it with one erotic memory seared into his brain. The top she wore hugged her lace-covered breasts and the jeans were so old and worn they fit her like a second skin. She looked demure, practical...and impossibly sexy.

He closed the distance between them. The sweet scent of lavender reached out to envelop him and Clayton would always associate that particular fragrance with Lucy and their first kiss. She placed her hand on his chest and looked up at him, her eyes wide, her breathing soft and erratic.

"One kiss, McKinley."

"It's a damn good start, Lucy."

She stood motionless as he kissed one cheek, then the other. His hands settled gently on her neck, his thumbs stroking over her chin and down her throat.

"McKinley…"

His eyes fixed on hers for a fraction of a second that seemed to last forever. There were no preliminaries, no hesitation or awkward uncertainty. There was only heat and passion.

He stroked his tongue over her bottom lip, releasing his grip on the last threads of rational thought as she opened her mouth to him on a sigh of pure surrender. Clayton denied her time to breathe, refused her time to think, deepening the kiss and urging her on when she met his tongue with her own.

The sounds she made, so soft and encouraging, sent fire racing through his body. She fit to him so perfectly, her breasts pressing against his chest. She was sweeter than he had ever guessed, and more of a temptation that he'd ever faced before. She was an addiction, in his blood now, surging through his veins.

Shy at first, Lucy finally took what she wanted from him, pouring herself into the kiss. She let herself go beneath his mouth, her body falling into his as she slipped her arms around his neck. His head dipped and his lips tasted her throat with a wet, openmouthed kiss.

Lucy pulled away, trembling, her hands clutching his shoulders, her breath coming in short bursts. She leaned her forehead against his chest. Her breasts felt heavy. Her nipples pushed against the lace of her bra and the sensation was almost unbearable. Every nerve ending in her body hummed with a desire she had only ever felt with him and a sharp arrow of need coiled in her womb.

"What...was that for?"

Clayton tried to get his own breathing back under control, loving the feel of her pressed against him so trustingly, his raging arousal nestled in the softness of her stomach. "That was because I can't be around you and not touch you," he replied, then his eyes narrowed and zeroed in on her own, the swirling amber depths threatening to pull him under. "I've wanted to do that ever since you marched your cute little behind into the Roadhouse that night. I want every single bloke here who will be looking at you to know that you're off limits."

Lucy had never believed in a man showing off a woman as some kind of prized possession. Now here he was staking his claim on her and she felt alive for the first time in her life. The fact that he wanted her so intensely unleashed something primitive inside her and she reveled in it.

"That's a very caveman thing to say, you know."

He shrugged, reaching up to brush away a strand of hair that had fallen onto her forehead. "It's appropriate then because my instincts are screaming for me to throw you over my shoulder, carry you off somewhere quiet and find out if this attraction between us is going to spark into the inferno I think it will."

If that kiss was anything to go by, the firestorm of desire would burn them alive. "Why me, McKinley?"

He ran his fingers through her hair, luxuriating in its softness, inhaling the floral scent of her shampoo. "Because you're feisty and funny. Because you care about those kids so much you'd give your life for any one of them. Because you're stubborn and independent and you drive me ten kinds of crazy, but most of all because you're you, Lucy."

"You could have said something about me being sexy enough to stop traffic," she said, managing a smile, though inside, her heart still beat like a drum.

"But you did, darlin'. On a lonely stretch of highway in the middle of nowhere you stopped me, and I haven't been able to get you out of my mind since."

Lucy shook her head. "I was joking."

"I'm not." he said, his look as direct as his words.

After giving her a kiss that all but burnt through the soles of her boots, Lucy couldn't believe he could be so calm. Her lips still felt as though they were on fire. She let her hands drop to her sides. Rational thought was impossible whenever she touched him. "Do you want to explain the activity out there in my yard?"

"It's a work party. We're here to build you a shed." When she would have protested he held up his hand. "And before you tell me again how you don't like charity, you should know that we've done this before when other people have been in a bind. It's tradition around here."

Lucy looked skeptical. "And someone just happened to donate all this material and food?"

Clayton grinned and rocked back on his heels. "As a matter of fact, it was donated. There are people in this town who think what you're doing is a good thing, Lucy. I told you before, we're not all like Gerry."

She thanked the Lord for that. "We'd better get back out there," she said, loath to give up the seclusion and privacy she wanted with him. "We'll go the back way," she said, handing him his hat.

His chuckle was deep and slow. "That might be best. You look like a wicked, wanton woman." When he raised their joined hands and brushed a soft kiss across her knuckles, time slowed to a crawl for her. The touch of his lips on her skin, the heated desire in his eyes as they remained locked with hers, the soft-as-a-whisper touch of his tongue as it licked over one of her fingers. He bombarded her senses to saturation point and Lucy couldn't believe how much she wanted to kiss him again.

"That's a becoming blush," he said, grinning. "Whatever were you thinking? I wonder."

They'd joined the other people congregated out back. Lucy wondered if anyone could tell what they'd been doing. "You ask too many questions."

Clayton smiled easily, tightening his grip on her fingers. "And you don't have nearly enough answers," he said. "People want to help you, Lucy. Let them do this for you. Enjoy yourself. I intend to."

Lucy watched the activity, gratitude welling inside her. "This was Katie's idea?"

He nodded. "She wanted to do something to make up for the fire. Shay suggested the work party." He came closer, taking her hand in his, his fingers smoothing over her skin in maddening circles. "Darlin', these people want to do this for you and the kids. Look at how much fun they're having."

Lucy did look, swallowing the knot of emotion that threatened to choke her. Thomas was helping Zach unload the roofing iron. Katie fussed over Molly, who wore tiny overalls the same colour as her father's, and Max ran around excitedly, determined to be a part of things.

Even Lisa talked shyly with a girl who looked to be about the same age. There were other children here too...it was a real family effort. And it was for them, thought Lucy, knowing her only option was to accept graciously.

Clayton wiggled her hand lightly and she looked back up at him. The breeze tousled his hair, and when he smiled he made her ache. The sensation startled her for a moment and though she felt embarrassed, she couldn't look away from him.

He set her senses burning and ignited everything feminine inside her. Clayton McKinley made her think of long nights and cool sheets, of making love until dawn.

"All right...you win," she said. "But don't get used to it. It won't happen too often."

"We'll see." Clayton plopped his hat on her head. "I don't want you getting sunburned."

Lucy smiled at his concern. "McKinley, it's not even a sunny day," she said, pointing to the overcast sky.

He shrugged. "Humour me."

She bit her lip to keep from smiling. "I guess it's the least I can do. You are helping to build me a new shed." She pointed him in the right direction. "Go to it."

He smiled and tweaked the end of her nose. "Don't accept invitations to sit with anyone for lunch...that's a date I intend to keep myself." Then he walked away, his backside as compact and alluring as she remembered it.

Lucy gave up trying to put him or the kiss out of her mind the rest of the morning, but she did manage to keep herself busy. There were so many people to meet and so much to do in preparation for lunch. Still he lingered on the periphery, causing her to look up every now and then from whatever she was doing, to glance at him. She took a deep breath. Twenty-five years old and now my libido decides to kick in, she thought ruefully.

Clayton watched her for the rest of the morning. He concentrated on the job at hand, but every few minutes or so his eyes would seek her out. She walked among the townsfolk, introducing herself to those she hadn't met, thanking the men who stopped to speak to her and answer her questions about the shed's construction. He didn't like the appreciative glances she was getting from some of the single men...and a few not so single. Damn it, jealousy had never been something he'd had to deal with before and he didn't like it one bit.

It was nearing lunchtime when Lucy looked up to see Angus Willoughby's police car cruise down her driveway. Since he was in uniform she knew he wasn't here to lend a hand. Wiping her hands on her jeans, she walked across to him, not surprised when Clayton caught up with her and fell into step beside her, saying nothing, but looking grim. Angus took off his cap and greeted them both, looking over to where the foundation of her shed was taking shape.

"They keep going like this you'll have your stables before sundown," he said, leaning back against his car. "It's about time this town did something to welcome you and the kids."

Lucy looked back to where the men were working. "This is the best welcome they could have given us."

Angus nodded, then his expression turned serious. "I thought you might like to know I've arrested Gerry Anderson for the arson attack on your stables."

Lucy swallowed, stunned for a moment, speechless. "How...I didn't think you found any evidence at the scene to link him to the fire."

"We didn't. I wondered why Gerry seemed to be favouring his arm the other day when I questioned him," he said, folding his arms across a massive chest. "He told me he'd had a fall from a horse. Turns out he's not a very accomplished arsonist. The fire got away from him. His father took him to the hospital last night. He's in a pretty bad way. He burned most of his arm, and since he didn't get it seen to right away, he'd picked up an infection."

Lucy frowned, trying to take it all in. "But you told me yesterday that his father gave him an alibi."

Angus squared his jaw. "When I reminded Davis of whose property was destroyed in the fire and the considerable legal weight Gray Harrison could bring down on them, he had a change of heart and remembered Gerry wasn't with him that night. With his alibi gone, Gerry confessed." He shook his head. "I don't think Davis knew anything about the fire until Gerry came home all burned."

Lucy knew it was cold comfort. "Are you going to charge Davis too?"

Angus nodded. "Accessory after the fact. Lying about Gerry being with him that night. He'll hire a smart lawyer to argue that he was only protecting his son. He'll probably get off with a caution but it might be enough to make him take a good hard look at what he's made of Gerry."

Clayton rubbed the back of Lucy's neck with his fingers, not surprised to feel tension knotting her muscles. "So it's over."

"Until the hearing anyway. That could be months away."

Lucy couldn't let go of the fear so easily though. "And in the meantime? What if he decides he's got nothing to lose since he's facing charges anyway?"

Angus shook his head. "Lucy, his arm was badly burned. The doctor is transferring him to the city today. He needs skin grafts...extensive ones. He won't be in any shape to cause trouble for you or anyone else for a long while." He looked up as someone called his name. "I'll just go and say hi to Connie."

When he was gone, Lucy just stood there, numb. She no longer had to worry that Gerry would bother them again, that the kids couldn't leave the house in safety or that leaving them on their own at the house while she ran errands was endangering them. Since the fire she had gone about the business of living each day, but in the back of her mind had been the constant fear that Gerry would strike again. Now that fear was gone and Lucy smiled...really smiled, feeling the tension leave her body in one great wave.

"I take it that smile means you're happy?"

She looked up at Clayton, shielding her eyes from the sun that was making its first appearance of the day. "I'd built Gerry up in my mind as this monster, and I didn't think we would ever be free of him. I wouldn't wish getting burned on anybody," she said, biting her lip. "But when I think of how he hurt Max, how arrogant he was toward me at the pub that night and then the fire..."

Clayton wanted to haul her against him and into his arms then and there, and kiss her in front of God and everyone. He reached out and brushed a strand of hair back from her face, tucking it gently behind her ear.

"It's over now," he said quietly. "You can live life with your children in peace." Then he smiled. "I'd better get back," he said, holding her hand up to his mouth and brushing a kiss into her palm. "I'll see you at lunch."

As lunchtime approached, Shay fired up the large portable barbecue someone had brought, and from the four-wheel drives came foldaway tables of every size and description, from card tables to picnic tables. Soon the aroma of sizzling meat permeated the air and by the time they laid down tools to eat, the sky had darkened slightly.

"I hope the rain holds off," said Lucy, setting out the salads on one of the tables.

"Elsie's arthritic leg isn't playing up, so I think we're safe," said Shay, loading up yet another hungry man's plate with meat and fried onion.

People utilized every surface. Some sat at the tables in folding chairs or stools. Others sat upon the bonnets of cars, but most found the green grass much more comfortable. Lucy provided blankets for them to sit on. At first she had watched in disbelief at the amount Shay piled onto each man's plate, but as the food disappeared and many of them come back for seconds, she merely smiled.

These men worked hard every day of their lives, Shay had told her. Lucy could see how seriously they took their food.

"The kids are having a ball," said Shay, pointing to a patch of grass where Katie and Max played and laughed with at least a dozen other children of all ages.

Thomas sat with a group of men, listening intently to every word, joining in when he had something to say. Lucy felt gratitude for what they were doing for him without their even realizing it. These men were making him feel as if he had something worthwhile to contribute to the discussion.

"Lisa seems to have found a friend."

Shay spied the two girls talking quietly on the porch steps over lunch. "That's Caroline Bingham. Her father's the mayor but she's staying with her aunt and uncle this weekend while her parents are away."

The conversation ended then as the last of the men, the McKinleys included, lined up for lunch. Once they were served what Lucy could only describe as mountainous portions of food, she got her own.

"You'll need more than a flimsy piece of steak." Clayton was behind her, his mouth close to her ear. "Grab a sausage and some baked 'taters."

Lucy purposely moved on to the salads. "I can't eat as much as you, McKinley."

"I don't want you wasting away to nothing."

Lucy laughed. "I doubt there's much chance of that."

Clayton frowned at her. "You say that like it's a bad thing."

Lucy's figure wasn't willowy. It never would be. Ever since her teenage years her curves had been there, a total antithesis of the model image pushed in magazines and movies of the modern woman. "Well, I'm never going to be skinny."

"Amen to that!" Clayton took her hand and led her to the back of his truck. He settled on the tray and held Lucy's plate while she did the same.

"You like matronly women?"

Clayton laughed as he passed her plate. "God, Lucy, there is nothing remotely matronly about you. What that cute backside of yours does to a pair of jeans should be illegal in every state." His eyes traveled the length of her body appreciatively and she felt them as if they were his hands. "You're the sexiest woman I've ever known."

Lucy didn't know what to say, and indeed never got the chance. "Why do you think I want you like a madman?" he asked, adding, "Apart from the fact that you're so irresistible."

Lucy ate some potato salad, smiling gamely. "Abstinence."

Clayton chuckled. "I handle abstinence just fine." He bit into a home-baked bread roll. "Opposites attract. I've been attracted to you since the night we met."

Chapter Seven

Lucy cast a covert look around, relieved to see that everyone else was too busy enjoying their lunch and the break to pay them any attention.

"That night in your kitchen just watching the delight you took in eating chocolate cake aroused me," he said, his smile growing as her eyes widened in shock. "The anticipation in your eyes, the way your tongue flicked out to catch a dab of chocolate on your lip. Now I'm aroused when you walk into a room, when I smell that fragrance you wear."

He grinned. "Most especially when you kiss me like you did this morning." He was pleased when her mouth fell open and her surprise and embarrassment registered as a blush. Finally he had her flustered, speechless. He also had her full attention and didn't intend to waste it. "I want to kiss you all over," he told her, his words as bold and deliberate as the look he gave her. "I want to start at the back of your neck and kiss my way down to your feet. Then I want to turn you over and kiss my way back up, tasting you, touching you.''

Lucy felt his words like the blast of a hot furnace. ''McKinley, please.''

''Oh, I want to please you, Lucy,'' he replied, his voice husky with intent as he purposely misunderstood her plea. ''And I'll take my time doing it.'' He put his plate on the bed of the truck between them and cupped her chin with his hand, forcing her to meet his gaze.

''I have to set a good example for the kids,'' she said, clutching at any straw to postpone this most intimate conversation.

He smiled. ''I wasn't suggesting I jump you on the couch one night in full view of them. But give them some credit. Katie's already guessed that I like you.''

Lucy looked aghast. ''She what?''

''She asked me not to hurt you. I promised her I wouldn't.'' He nudged her gently, his elbow brushing her ribs. ''Come out with me tonight, Lucy.''

''Tonight?''

''I'm sure Thomas wouldn't mind baby-sitting. Or in a pinch we could get Shay to stay with the kids.''

Lucy bit her bottom lip, wondering if there was any obstacle this man didn't just blast out of his path. ''Thomas can handle it,'' she assured him. ''I just don't want them to get the wrong idea.''

''About us?''

She nodded. ''Stability is something they need in their lives.''

Clayton placed his knuckles beneath her chin and turned her face to his. ''Us going out won't traumatize them, Lucy,'' he said, his eyes locked with hers. ''I guarantee you'll have fun.''

He left her sitting there as he ditched his empty plastic plate into a garbage bag and went back to work.

Five minutes later everyone was toiling once again. The next time she saw him, he had his shirt off. Other men had discarded their shirts as well but he was the only man she had eyes for. He really was beautifully built, exuding a strength that went beyond the physical, a sense that he could accomplish anything he wanted to.

It was mesmerizing watching the muscles ripple in his back, seeing his strong shoulders take the strain when he helped another man lift a long, heavy beam. His arms were toned and powerful, his torso a washboard of muscle, and sweat glistened on his bronzed skin. His wide, smooth chest drew her attention and Lucy found her gaze drawn to the wedge of dark hair that began at his navel and arrowed down to disappear beneath the belt of his jeans.

When Lucy let her eyes make the return journey, she found him standing straight and tall, staring back at her. Twenty feet separated them but his slow, seductive smile bridged the gap and touched her like a bold, erotic caress. She swallowed, dragging her eyes away. After that she avoided looking in his direction when he might catch her doing it. Instead, she joined the women as they packed leftovers into Lucy's fridge, despite her protests that they should take the food home.

Once the kitchen was clean they went outside to watch construction and taking a much-needed supply of drink-filled coolers with them. The older children made themselves useful fetching and carrying for the men while the younger ones played in the shade of a giant eucalypt.

Lucy was folding the last table when Shay came over and handed her a frosted glass of homemade lemonade. "All I can say is we're lucky it isn't bushfire season."

Lucy frowned. "Why?"

Shay sipped her drink. "That smile Clayton just gave you sent off enough sparks to light a dozen spot fires."

"He's trying to unnerve me."

Shay chuckled. "Dragging you into the laundry this morning was probably a strategic first strike."

"That was unexpected and embarrassing."

"Most things with Clayton usually are," she said dryly, dropping into one of the folding chairs that sat in the shade. "Unexpected, I mean...not embarrassing."

Lucy settled herself in the other chair. "He asked me out tonight."

Shay stretched out and smiled. "And you look as though you're thinking about it." She whistled appreciatively. "That must have been some interlude in the laundry."

Lucy looked down at the glass in her hand and shrugged. "It was just a kiss."

"Using the phrase 'just a kiss' when referring to Clayton would probably earn you the scorn of most single women in this town," she said conspiratorially. "You looked shellshocked when you came back out."

Lucy groaned and felt nauseated. "You could tell...what we'd been doing?"

Shay reached over and touched her hand comfortingly. "Don't worry. General consensus is that the two of you look good together."

General consensus didn't worry her. The feelings he aroused in her did. "What he did this morning will give the gossips grist for their mill until the cows come home sometime next spring."

Shay threw back her head and laughed. "Not to mention inciting all the single women in town who have tried to land him in the past to riot."

"I haven't landed him," Lucy stressed. "I don't want to land him. We're just friends." *God, how she wanted it to be true.*

Shay leaned forward. "Did Clayton tell you where all the materials came from to build the shed?" Lucy shook her head. "He knew you wouldn't accept it if he just went out and paid for everything himself, so he petitioned the local council."

"I...I don't understand. What does the council have to do with this?"

"They have an emergency fund that they use to help out any nonprofit organization in town," she said, smiling softly. "Clayton went to the meeting Thursday night and persuaded them that Harrison House would be deserving of a little of that money to rebuild the shed you lost."

Lucy was stunned. "When he said it had been donated I thought maybe Gray had something to do with it." She looked over to where Clayton stood, shielding his eyes from the glare of the sun while he gave directions to Josh on the placement of a beam. "He said it was Katie's idea."

Shay settled back in her chair again. "It was her idea to get the townspeople to help out. We did that together."

Lucy sighed. "I was determined to keep him out of my life, not to let him get too close."

Shay smiled. "Do you think your brood might like to have dinner at our place and then catch a movie in town with Molly and me?"

Lucy shot her a grateful look. "I think they'd jump at the chance," she said, butterflies the size of dive-bombers loose in her stomach. "Thank you."

"You're welcome, Lucy. Just do me one favour." Lucy nodded. "Have a great time."

The sun was kissing the hills, painting them a lustrous shade of purple when Lucy thanked the last couple as they left. She had made a point not to let anyone get away without thanking them for their kindness and her brand-new shed.

Katie came up and hugged her. "Today was great."

"Thanks to your wonderful idea."

She shrugged, a little embarrassed. "You deserve good things, Lucy. We all do."

Lisa waved goodbye to Caroline and her family then wandered over to where Lucy stood. "Seems like you made a friend," she commented.

The girl rolled her eyes, her smile grim. "Yeah, she's okay, I guess. Her father's the mayor so he'll be over the moon about her being friends with me."

"Give them a chance, Lisa."

She gave Lucy a world-weary look. "A chance to do what? Look down on me? Decide I'm not good enough to be friends with Caroline?"

"They might just surprise you."

Lisa shrugged as if she couldn't care less, as if it didn't matter to her whether or not she managed a friendship with the girl, but Lucy could see in her eyes that she desperately wanted it. Thomas and Max joined them at the veranda steps, the younger boy barely able to contain his excitement.

"I might be on Mr. Wilson's soccer team, Lucy. He said I could try out when school went back."

She ruffled his hair. "Good for you."

Thomas motioned toward the McKinleys, who were packing the last of the tables and trays into the back of their truck. "Shay invited us for dinner tonight. Then she's taking Molly to a movie so Josh can get caught up with his paperwork. She thought we might like to go. How about you?"

Lucy took a deep breath and looked at each one of them, her gaze coming to rest on Thomas. "Actually, I've been asked out tonight."

Katie squealed. "A date? You're going on a date?"

Lucy nodded. "If I can still remember how it's done."

Thomas looked resigned. "You going out with Mc-Kinley?"

"Yeah, I am," she said, relieved when he merely nodded.

"Good, at least now we might have a chance to talk Shay into watching something better than that movie you took us to in the city last year."

Lucy smiled at Max. Trust him to have his priorities right. "It wasn't that bad."

Max rolled his eyes. "Every woman left the place in tears, including you three," he said, giving pointed glances to Lisa and Katie as well.

Katie looked down her nose at him. "Well, at least the death toll didn't exceed the population of a small country."

Lucy smiled at the byplay. "How about you all go get cleaned up?"

Max and Katie ran for dibs on the bathroom. Thomas gave her a measuring look. "You deserve some time for yourself," he said finally. "Just don't do anything I wouldn't do," he told her, a slight knowing smile on his face, the same smile he'd tried to hide when she'd given her safe-sex lectures at the refuge. "And if you do, make sure you don't get caught."

Lucy was still grinning when he went inside. "How do you feel about it, Lisa?"

"Like I really don't want to know what it is you might get caught doing." She wrinkled her nose. "I didn't think old people did that kind of thing."

Lucy chuckled. "Gee, thanks very much. I suppose you'll be getting me a walking frame for Christmas, too."

"Oh, you know what I mean."

"We're going out, Lisa, that's all."

The girl looked skeptical. "You'll be careful though, you know, if he wants to…"

"I'll be fine." She pointed toward the steps. "You'd better go stand in line for the bathroom or you'll never get in, the way they go back and forth all the time."

Lucy watched her go and was startled when a tapping on her shoulder had her spinning on her heel. Clayton had put his shirt back on, and his jeans and boots were covered in sawdust. But even sweaty, dirty and with a slight five o'clock shadow beginning to darken his jawline, he was enough to tempt all the angels in heaven to turn in their halos and trade in their wings just for the chance to be mortal again.

"I wish you wouldn't sneak up on me."

He grinned. "So, I hear you're free tonight. Got any plans?"

Lucy stood with her hands planted firmly on her hips. Just because she was going to give in and go out with him didn't mean she was going to make it easy for him. "You know, gloating is highly unattractive."

"I'll take the risk," he said, taking hold of her hand. "How do the kids feel about it?"

Lucy chuckled. "Max is relieved I won't have a say in the movie he gets to see. Katie's ecstatic and Lisa thinks I'm too old to be doing what Thomas thinks I'm going to be doing with you.''

Clayton laughed, enjoying the moment and the woman he was sharing it with. ''Ah, darlin', you're never too old. I'll pick you up at seven, that should give us both enough time to get ready.''

''How should I dress? Are we going formal?''

''It's a surprise.'' He looked down her body appreciatively and Lucy fought the urge to squirm. ''Jeans or a dress...the choice is yours.''

Lucy feigned gratitude. ''At last I get a choice in something.'' She heard his chuckle as he walked away and couldn't suppress a tiny smile as she went inside.

She knew the minute she opened the front door to him that evening that by dressing in a denim skirt that ended an inch above her knees she had made his night. If the grin on his far-too-handsome face hadn't made it clear, the died-and-gone-to-heaven look in his eyes would have. She had teamed the skirt with a plain white, sleeveless blouse that buttoned down the front and tucked into the waistband at her hips. She'd left her hair down, using a brush and her hair dryer to give it the fullness and bounce only time and patience could achieve.

''I knew beneath those jeans and baggy track pants there was a spectacular set of legs.'' He surveyed her from head to toe and back again. With just a slight touch of makeup and her hair fluffed and falling softly around her shoulders, she took his breath away. ''You are one gorgeous lady.''

''Thank you,'' she said, blushing all over again.

She slipped into her flat-heeled shoes and gave him a wry look, noting the way his jeans hugged trim hips, how his blue chambray shirt hugged those shoulders she'd coveted earlier. Even the boots on his feet had been polished to a shine. "You look very...masculine."

He smiled, looking pleased with himself. "Well, that's the look I was aiming for," he said, closing the distance between them before dipping his head to take her mouth in a kiss that threatened to take possession of her soul. Lucy hung on to him, her hands at his waist, clutching denim. With one last erotic sweep of his tongue in her mouth, he ended the kiss and pulled back. "If we don't leave now we won't leave at all."

Lucy heeded the sensual warning. Part of her wanted to throw caution to the wind and lead him upstairs. Another part of her, the practical part, told her she wasn't ready to take that step with him yet.

"Let's go."

She got to choose where they ate dinner. Seeing as the options were limited to a hamburger joint, a pizza parlour and one fine-dining restaurant, they ended up sitting at a corner booth in the busy pizzeria licking cheese off their fingers and arguing over who had the better topping.

"Anchovies make the pizza."

Lucy shot him a disgusted look. "You're a sick man, McKinley. How can you eat anything that resembles stray eyebrows and tastes like something from the Dead Sea? Don't you care what you put into your body?"

He took a sip of ice-cold beer and gave her a wry grin. "This from the woman whose cholesterol level is probably higher than the Australian foreign debt."

The waitress sauntered over then. There was just no other word to describe her hip-swiveling display, Lucy decided. It was as if Lucy had ceased to exist, for the woman had eyes only for Clayton.

"Hi, Clay. Can I get you anything else?"

Clay? Lucy watched him turn his usual thousand-watt smile on the waitress and promptly witnessed her transformation into a giggling, flirting man-magnet. "You might box up what's left of these two pizzas for us, Minnie."

Her come-get-me smile wavered for a second. When she didn't get the attention from him she had obviously been expecting, she picked up the trays, cast a withering glance at Lucy that would have sent her to the morgue if looks could kill and walked away, the hips not so noticeable now.

"Minnie?"

Clayton finished his beer. "Minette Harvey. We went to school together."

"And you dated her."

He shot her a look of surprise. "How did you know?"

"Oh, please! The woman looks at you like she knows what she's missing." From the snug uniform and the pouting red lips, to the way she swept her hair off her neck and shook it down her back, the woman oozed sex. "She's every man's fantasy."

"She's not my fantasy, Lucy, and don't you forget it. Besides, it was a few years ago now that we dated. I was superseded by a guy with an MG convertible and an apartment in the city."

Lucy arched an eyebrow. "Gee, now that's what I call a solid foundation for a relationship."

"If memory serves me correctly, a relationship wasn't high on Minette's list of priorities." He leaned closer and grinned. "Jealous?"

Of course she was jealous and that irritated her. It was irrational and totally uncalled for yet she felt it anyway.

"I'm just amazed men actually fall for that wide-eyed, giggly bombshell routine."

He agreed, the solemn look on his face not fooling her for a second. "Yeah, I don't know what I could have been thinking when I went out with her."

Lucy pulled a paper napkin from the dispenser and wiped her fingers one by one. "I could probably hazard a guess as to what you were thinking *with*. Men don't need to think when they go out with women as gorgeous as Minnie," she said, no malice in her voice and just a tinge of envy for the sexual confidence the woman exuded. "They put their brains in neutral and let their hormones do the driving."

Did she think she wasn't as sexy as Minnie? Well, he'd just have to prove to her how beautiful she was. Telling her wasn't having the slightest effect, and hell, there were times when actions spoke louder than words. He stood and reached into the back pocket of his jeans for his wallet then held out his hand to her. Lucy took his hand and they walked up to the cash register. The blonde ignored Lucy until Clayton introduced her.

"You're the one with all those kids at the Harrison place." When Lucy nodded, Minnie looked at her as if she were insane. "Why on earth would you want to take on the job of raising someone else's kids?" she asked, making it sound as though the practice should be outlawed.

"It's not for everyone," said Lucy, trying to be charitable. "Do you have children?"

Minnie took Clayton's money and gave him change. "You've got to be joking. Look, honey, this figure is hard enough to keep without getting pregnant. Kids are like wrinkles...with you for life."

Lucy bit back the razor-sharp retort that hovered on

her lips. With people like Minnie, a dictionary full of words didn't change their opinions. "Well, it was nice to meet you."

"Yeah. We might even get together and compare notes when good old love-'em-and-leave-'em McKinley here moves on," she said, casting a look at him that was tinged with longing and bitterness.

Clayton put his wallet back in his pocket. "Oh, I don't think Lucy has to worry about that, Minnie," he said, raising Lucy's hand to his mouth for a kiss, his eyes fixed on her. "She's a beautiful woman with a great bunch of kids. What more could a man want?"

Minnie's mouth dropped open. Lucy stared at him as if he had lost his mind completely. Clayton picked up the pizza boxes. "You have a nice evening, Minnie."

Lucy held her tongue until they were sitting in Clayton's truck. "Do you know what she's thinking right now?"

He chuckled and started the engine. "Nothing too deep, I imagine."

"She's thinking we're a couple. You made it sound like we've done everything but book the church!"

"Is that all you're worried about? I thought you might want to ask me if I'm really a love-'em-and-leave-'em type of bloke."

Lucy didn't have to ask. "She's hurt, McKinley. A woman scorned and all that."

"But she's the one who dumped me."

"Lust knows no logic," she told him. "Obviously she's realizing her mistake." But Lucy couldn't help wondering how intimate their relationship had been. Had they…no! She wasn't even going there. What he had done before was nothing to do with her.

"Stop biting your lip and ask me what's got you so deep in thought."

Lucy looked out the windscreen and shook her head, wishing he wasn't so observant. He reached over and turned her face toward his. When he looked at her so possessively she found it hard to think. "You're wondering if I slept with her."

"I have no right to ask you anything like that."

She had more right than she knew, Clayton thought. "I want to tell you." He searched her face and slowly, a warm toe-tingling smile appeared on his lips. "I won't pretend there haven't been women, Lucy. But Minnie and I were never lovers."

Lucy didn't deserve to feel so relieved. No wonder the woman was upset. "Are we going home now or do you have something else in mind?"

He had a lot in mind but for now they were going to have some fun. "Go home? I do know how to show a lady a good time. I'm taking you dancing."

Lucy chuckled. "I'm about as comfortable on the dance floor as I am on a horse."

He raised an eyebrow at her. "Is that another challenge, darlin'?"

She shot him a dry look. "No, McKinley. I don't make the same mistakes twice." she said, trying to ignore his cocky, devilishly sexy grin. When they pulled into the parking lot of the Roadhouse fifteen minutes later Lucy cringed. "I still can't believe I just waltzed in there and hauled Gerry over the coals in front of people." She glanced at him. "Tell me it wasn't crowded."

"Oh, darlin', on a Saturday night with all the farmhands in town the day after payday?" He reached across and brushed a strand of hair from her face. "They even stopped the music to listen to you."

Now *that* she did remember. Lucy slumped back in her seat, eyeing the door with irritation. "Me and my big mouth."

He leaned over, kissing her ear, startling her into turning toward him. "I happen to like your mouth," he said, and then he proceeded to show her just how much. All Lucy could do was thread her fingers into his hair and clutch at his shoulder with the other one. His tongue made a sweep of her mouth, meeting her own in a playful duel before he pulled away.

It took her a moment to catch her breath. "McKinley, when they had show-and-tell at school did you ever just settle for telling?"

Clayton grinned, coming around to her side of the truck and helping her out. "Physical displays are so much more effective." He took her hand in his and they walked toward the double oak doors. The music hit them the minute they were inside. Lucy looked around, really seeing the place for the first time. Smoke hung in the air, people were trying to talk above the music and the employees behind the bar were run off their feet. The band was good, Lucy decided, her foot tapping to the rhythm.

"Isn't this great?"

Lucy looked up at him, realizing he was in his element here. "At least nobody has to worry about making conversation," she said, raising her voice to be heard. He smiled and led her away from the band, toward the bar.

"We'll get a table near the back where it's not so loud," he said. "Drink?"

"Orange juice, thanks."

He nodded and turned back to the bartender, giving their order. When he had paid for the drinks, he handed Lucy hers and led the way to a table in the far corner.

"I can remember the first time I came here," he said, his eyes bright and dancing. "I'd just turned eighteen and was aiming to go parking with this girl I had my eye on."

Lucy sipped her drink. "It's hard to imagine you ever being eighteen."

He smiled. "Well, for a while there I thought I'd never get any older. But then I guess it's a folly of youth to want everything at once."

"I can barely remember what it was like to be eighteen," she said, stirring her drink with the straw. "I was studying for my Higher School Certificate and trying to choose a university."

Clayton watched her, the expression on her face more resigned than sad. "Your family must be proud of you."

She smiled, but it was cold. "I don't know, I can't imagine they give it much thought. My mother is always busy with one of her charities and my father is head of the ECHO communications network."

Clayton was stunned. "Elliot Warner? He's one of the wealthiest men in the country."

Lucy nodded. "I think he came in at number three last year," she said, as if she were discussing the weather.

Clayton frowned. "You seemed so reluctant to discuss your past or your family, I assumed you'd had a life similar to the kids you work with."

She looked down at the Formica tabletop. "It would have been better for all concerned if I had."

"Did they hurt you, Lucy?"

She smiled sadly. "No, McKinley. I had everything I could want. The best schools. Tutors. A first-rate education. I mingled with Sydney's elite social set and never had to worry where my next meal was coming from or if I'd have a warm bed for the night.''

Clayton studied her, watching the way her eyes clouded over, the way she traced invisible patterns on the table. "But you weren't happy.''

"I should have been. At first I was rebellious,'' she said. "I hated the fact that everything I did, Daphne—my mother—saw as a reflection on her as a parent. I didn't concentrate on school and I was such a tomboy she gave up any hope of getting me into a dress once I'd turned seven.''

Clayton traced her knuckles with his finger. "Sounds like you were a typical kid.''

"I was stubborn and willful and destined for trouble...or so our priest told me once.'' Unfortunately the words had proved too accurate for comfort.

"Did you have a falling-out with your family?''

Lucy took a sip of orange juice and met his intent gaze. "Yes. At the time I thought it was the end of the world.'' And it had been. But it had also marked the beginning of her new life. She'd buried the old Lucy with Megan. The one who would act on impulse, without thinking. The girl who did whatever her parents told her not to just to make them notice her. From that moment on she'd been a model daughter, a straight-A student, but none of it would ever make up for one moment of recklessness.

"And now?'' he asked, watching her carefully.

"Now I don't know if I will ever be close to them again.''

Chapter Eight

Clayton sensed a sadness in her that he had only touched on here tonight. Lucy deserved anything but to be sad. He didn't push, or ask more questions. The fact that she'd volunteered as much information as she had was more than he'd expected. "Dance with me."

She grinned. "Are your toes insured?"

"I trust you with all my body parts, Lucy."

He stood and held out his hand to her. He counted her hesitation in seconds and got to five before she laid her hand in his. His fingers closed around hers and he pulled her with him toward the dance floor.

Couples clapped enthusiastically to the last bars of a fast two-step. She was about to protest that two-stepping was outside her very basic dance abilities, but then the band struck the first haunting chords of a soft, slow love song and she offered no resistance when he pulled her into his arms.

Lucy closed her eyes, allowing her other senses to soak up the moment. The smell of his woodsy after-

shave. The feel of his calm, warm breath teasing past
her ear. His arm went around her, the palm of his hand
pressed to the small of her back firmly while he rested
their joined hands against his chest. The music wrapped
around her, etching this moment in her mind forever.

Clayton pulled her close to him, his hand at her back
coaxing her body toward his until his arousal brushed
against the softness of her stomach. He took a deep
breath and realized just how damn long it had been since
he'd craved the touch of a woman like he did Lucy's
touch. It felt good. Hell, it felt better than good. It felt
right. Everything about Lucy felt right to him. Her
breasts pressed to his chest, the lavender scent that en-
veloped him. The way she hesitated for a fraction of a
second before allowing herself to melt against him completely.

He rested his chin lightly near her temple and closed
his eyes, savouring the moment and the woman. The
words of the song wrapped around him. She tilted her
head back and looked up at him with those amber eyes
and his gaze dropped to her mouth, luscious and kiss-
able…just as it had been this morning. If this was a test
then he was going to crumble in the face of temptation
for sure.

They danced that song and several after that. For the
next hour Clayton encouraged Lucy to be adventurous
with the faster songs, twirling her around, swinging her
out and back into his arms.

Then another slow song would start and she would
find herself wrapped in his arms and wishing she could
just stay there forever. The atmosphere seeped into her
bones and she fell under the spell of the music and the
man holding her. When she tilted her head back and

looked up at him he was watching her with an intensity that touched her deep inside.

"I want to take you home, Lucy."

At home they would be alone and suddenly she wanted that, wanted whatever brief moments she could steal with him, if only just for tonight. "Let's go."

The drive back to Lucy's was filled with a silence neither felt compelled to put an end to. From the moment he'd gotten into the truck Clayton had held her hand on his thigh, her palm pressed softly to the denim of his jeans. She felt heat and power, muscle and strength. And suddenly she wanted to touch him as he had touched her this morning, with determination and a single-mindedness that left no room for doubts.

When they pulled into the yard, she didn't wait for him to come around and open her door and was to the veranda before his long-legged strides caught up with her. The car wasn't parked in its usual place, which meant the kids were still out.

Lucy swallowed the giant-size lump of indecision that welled in her and unlocked the door. He followed her inside and she watched him shrug out of his jacket and lay it over the arm of the easy chair in the corner before coming toward her with slow, certain steps.

He cupped her cheek, his fingers cool on her warm skin, and Lucy lost herself in eyes that were suddenly the blue of a storm-filled sky. He stroked his thumb over the skin of her jaw and Lucy was helplessly, hopelessly caught when his gaze lingered on her lips before rising to her eyes.

"I have never wanted anything in my life as much as I want you, Lucy."

And she believed every word he spoke. Her hands gripped his strong forearms as his head bent to hers.

Lucy thought she was ready for his kiss but nothing this side of heaven could have prepared her for the reality of such out-of-control desire. She gave up thinking and lost herself in pure, raw sensation.

He wrapped his arms around her and pulled her to him so they touched from chest to thigh and kissed her again, his tongue teasing her, tasting her. His big, capable hands were infinitely tender even in their fevered haste, smoothing up her arms and down to cover her breasts. Then he took the sensual onslaught into high gear and pressed openmouthed kisses to her throat, his tongue leaving a deliciously moist trail.

Lucy slid her arms around his neck as her body gave in to the urge to move against his in an age-old rhythm. Too close would never be close enough. When he walked her backward to the couch Lucy clung to him, wanting everything and wanting it right now.

Clayton had known they would be a perfect fit in every way, but now the possibilities had him going out of his mind. He gave her time to object, time to tell him to stop but she wanted neither, and when he fell down onto the couch he brought her with him. But at the last second she moved her body to straddle his hips with her thighs and Clayton wondered if this was heaven.

When she settled herself on him he watched her eyes widen at the strength of his arousal. Some corner of his mind feared she would come to her senses and tell him it was a mistake. Every sense he had prayed that she didn't. And then she smiled, and any doubts he had vanished. Like a man lost in a world where only pleasure mattered, he ran his fingers through her hair, the silken mass soft and fragrant.

"This is better than standing up," she said, her voice husky, her breathing choppy.

"Darlin', this is better than just about anything I can think of," he replied as his fingers worked at the buttons on her blouse.

"If you're still thinking I'm doing something wrong."

His chuckle was strained, his hands trembling until finally her blouse lay open. "You haven't done anything wrong since we walked in the front door," he said, turning his attentions to her body, to her pleasure.

The plain cotton bra she wore could not have been sexier if it had been made of the finest silk and lace. He kissed the swell of one breast, then the other, ignoring the front clasp for now. Through the material he scored her nipples with his tongue until they peaked diamond hard. Her breathless plea for him to do it again thrilled him.

Lucy's breath came in short, sharp puffs. Soft sounds came from her as she tangled her hand in his hair. He tasted her again and again, pulling back every few seconds to make eye contact with her, watching the pleasure he was bringing her, the same pleasure that had him fired up like a rocket ready to launch. With lips and tongue he scalded her collarbone, her shoulders.

"You are a truly beautiful woman, Lucy."

She looked at him, her eyes drowsy with passion, her lips swollen and slightly parted. "I'm glad you think so. You make me feel beautiful," she replied, her voice a mere whisper. "You make me feel...everything."

His lips and hands played over her upper body where before tonight only his imagination had been allowed. Before Clayton could reach up and smooth the blouse off her shoulders she did it for him with a subtle shrug of her shoulders.

Lucy had never felt more exposed, more vulnerable than she did under his heated gaze. The only sound was their ragged gasps for air. She drew her hands up his chest and began on the buttons of his shirt, needing to touch him, to pleasure him as he was doing to her.

"Please, McKinley…"

He raised his head a fraction, meeting her eyes. "You want me to stop?"

"God, no!"

She got his shirt open in the same second that he dispensed with the clasp on her bra. He brushed it away from her body, awed with the gift of trust she was giving him. Her breasts were lush and full, just right for his hands, her nipples a dusty-rose hue peaked for his attention.

Lucy sucked in her breath at the first touch of his mouth on her breast, laving the nipple until just the scrape of his tongue across it was a pleasure that bordered on pain. All her life she had thought her breasts too ample, but Clayton paid homage to them so sweetly, his eyes a darker, swirling blue and filled with sexual intent.

Lucy felt perfect beneath his callused but expert hands and his talented mouth. She wondered if anyone had ever died of this much pleasure and then began to wonder how on earth she could have gone without this for so long. He moved his body slowly up hers until he was looking down into eyes of hot amber. With a slight tilt of his hips his arousal nestled more firmly into the V of her thighs and he watched her eyes close on a sigh.

"Oh, McKinley…"

"What do I have to do to hear you call me Clayton?"

Lucy opened her eyes and gave him a wicked smile. "You're a clever man. I'm sure you'll think of something," she said, sealing her lips to his.

Lucy took control and learned how to kiss him until

he moaned. Her hands ran over his smooth chest, stopping to play over his small nipples ever so briefly, thrilling in her abilities to bring him pleasure when he sucked in a startled breath. She was so drugged with the possibilities, so caught up in the man, the emotions and the moment that she stiffened at his blunt, vivid curse.

"What is it? What did I—" But before she even finished the sentence, she was being lifted off him to stand on unsteady legs as the sound of an insistent car horn evaporated the sensual haze. "The kids!"

Thank God for Thomas, Lucy thought. He'd obviously seen Clayton's truck and that the lights were out. He was a teenage boy on the brink of adulthood and he wouldn't be easily fooled. Sounding the horn was his way of giving them enough time to get themselves together. Of course, how she'd look him in the eye was another matter altogether. She hurriedly fixed her clothes, refastening her bra and blouse before tucking it into her skirt.

Clayton rebuttoned his shirt and tucked the tails hastily into jeans that felt about three sizes too small. He hoped like hell he could escape into the kitchen and get his body back under some control before the older kids figured out exactly what they'd been doing, though he'd guess Thomas already had a fair idea.

Smoothing her hair down, Lucy glanced at him.

"Well? How do I look?"

Clayton chuckled. "You look like a wickedly sexy woman. Your lips are swollen and full of colour, not to mention the fact that you're blushing nicely. I don't think we're gonna fool them, darlin'."

"Great! That's just the impression I want to give four nosy teenagers," she said dryly. "You go make the coffee and I'll do my best to handle damage control."

He caressed her cheek and brushed a quick kiss across her lips even as he heard the engine stop and a car door slam. "No regrets?"

Her smile was tentative. "None."

"Then that's a damn good start."

"I can't believe they went to bed so easily," Lucy remarked later as she perched herself on a kitchen chair. Max and Katie had both been stifling yawns and fighting exhaustion to tell her about the movie, while Lisa had looked at her with shy speculation and Thomas had grinned with a far-too-knowing expression. They'd each popped their head in to say good-night to Clayton, but Thomas had ushered them upstairs pretty quickly. If she ever got over her embarrassment she might thank him.

Clayton looked around from pouring coffee. "Thomas didn't say anything?"

Lucy grinned. "He didn't have to. He has this way of giving you just a look…and it says more than a thousand words ever could."

He came back to the table carrying two mugs of steaming hot coffee. When she took a sip and winced he smiled. "Hot?"

"Awful!"

"I happen to think I make a great cup."

"Well, think again, McKinley. They could use this stuff to embalm the dead."

He looked wounded, which of course she knew was for her benefit. "There are some things I do exceptionally well and I've been told making coffee is right up there at the top of the list."

Lucy refused to be embarrassed with him and it seemed rather ridiculous, given what they had been doing twenty minutes ago. "I'll admit you have hidden talents," she said, biting back a smile. "But trust me on this, I know bad coffee when I taste it." She stirred an extra teaspoon of sugar into her cup, sipping experimentally. Well, that was drinkable.

"Since taking up where we left off is out of the question," she said, "would you tell me what your parents were like?"

Raised eyebrows were the only sign she'd surprised him, then he smiled, slow and sweet. "They were ordinary people with an extraordinary love. They could be in a room together and just look at each other. It was like watching something magical." He chuckled. "When Dad rodeoed he used to joke with his mates that it would take a miracle to get him to the altar."

"And your mother was his miracle." Lucy wondered what it would be like to be loved like that.

He nodded. "I was twelve when she died. They diagnosed her cancer too late," he said quietly. "Dad was lost without her. He was like a building with the foundations ripped from underneath."

Lucy felt for the boy he'd been then and wondered how she would react if she lost her parents. "Her death must have been hard on you being so young."

He shrugged. "It was tough on all of us. But Dad crawled into the grave with her...except his coffin was a bourbon bottle and he stayed there for a year."

Lucy could picture him as a boy, caught up in his own grief and seeing his father's pain. "It sounds as if they had a once-in-a-lifetime love."

"They sure did. Dad went to hell and back that first year. His grief was so real you could almost touch it. On the first anniversary of her death he went out to the cemetery and stayed there until noon. He told us later he'd been saying goodbye." He took a mouthful of coffee and looked thoughtful. "Dad never touched another drink. I don't think he ever got over her death and he never even looked at another woman. He died when I was twenty-two."

Lucy swallowed past the lump in her throat. To be loved like that, so deeply that not even death could break the ties. "I'm sorry I'll never meet them." To her they sounded like good people, the kind she would have liked. "I imagine they're proud of all three of their sons."

He shrugged and smiled down at her. "I like to think so." He chuckled softly. "When I saw what Dad went through I thought loving someone that much was crazy. There didn't seem to be any sense to it, just pain and heartache when it ended."

"And now?" she asked, holding her breath and hoping he wouldn't say the words.

"Now I'm older and I can look back on all the years they had together. I can see the magic, remember the unbelievable happiness they gave each other. They didn't just love each other...they were in love," he said, his words more powerful for the emotion that accompanied them.

Lucy wasn't surprised. She'd seen him with his family, with her kids. He was sweet and sexy and charming. But more than that he had a strong sense of commitment to family and his heritage. If ever there was a man women would line up to marry, he was it. Still, hearing him say the words had brought her predicament home to her with a jolt. He was planning a future she couldn't be a part of, but after the evening they'd just spent together Lucy didn't want to give him up.

Would Megan hate her for taking happiness where she

could find it? Lucy honestly didn't think she deserved a man like Clayton in her life.

"Lucy?"

She looked into the eyes she dreamed about at night, at the mouth she'd kissed. Down at his hands, now wrapped around the coffee mug, hands he had touched her body with, hands that had moved over her bare skin with such tenderness.

The telephone rang then and Lucy breathed a sigh of relief and excused herself, leaving him in the kitchen as she walked into the living room. It was Zach calling to let Clayton know that his favourite mare had just gone into labour. It touched her deep inside to see the instant concern in his eyes for an animal. That caring spilled over into everything he did, she realized. It made him who he was. A man she could so easily fall in love with. He shrugged into his jacket minutes later and she walked him to the door.

"Thank you for this evening, McKinley. I had fun."

He grinned. "So did I. Maybe we can do it again."

"Dinner and dancing?" asked the imp inside her.

Clayton chuckled. "That too," he replied before pulling her close for a deep, passion-filled kiss and a reluctant groan as he stepped back. "I'll see you tomorrow for another riding lesson."

"Will you kiss me again?"

"You can bet on it."

With a smile, she promised him she'd be there at midday and Clayton left her standing at the door.

The week that followed was one Lucy would always look back on with fondness. Max, Katie and Lisa started school, the older girl showing more enthusiasm than Lucy had been expecting. Of course, the fact that Caroline's parents seemed accepting of her had helped enormously. Thomas kept himself busy around the farm and slowly but surely it was beginning to resemble the kind of place Lucy had envisaged.

Shay had invited them all to dinner two nights in a row and then Lucy had returned the favour, the kids excited to be cooking dinner for the McKinleys. And Clayton…well, he was always there in her life somehow. Her riding lessons proved little more than foreplay, the stolen hours they spent down at the creek were the only times they could be alone. Yet their tender moments were as intense as the night on her couch, both agreeing that absolute intimacy was better learned in slow, easy stages.

It was Sunday night, two weeks after Clayton McKinley had walked into her life that Lucy realized how important he was becoming to her.

He'd come over for dinner and now, with the kids in bed and the house quiet, he was showing her the grainy sepia photographs that chronicled his family's history.

Lucy sipped her coffee and couldn't help a smile when old photos gave way to slightly more recent ones. They laughed at photos showing him and his brothers as tearaway kids, enjoying life on the farm, and she didn't miss the softening in his voice when he pointed out the ones of his parents. The love was there, Lucy thought. In each photograph. In each look captured for eternity it was visible.

When the telephone rang Lucy was reluctant to drag herself away from the nostalgic journey through the McKinley past but she did.

Clayton watched her go, never having seen her more at ease, more completely relaxed and animated as tonight. He thought back on the last seven days and tried to remember when his self-control had ever endured a workout like the one it was getting with Lucy. The thrill of learning what pleased her, the sounds she made when they indulged in harmless foreplay, these things drove him out of his mind as never before.

He tipped his chair back onto two legs and peeked around the door at her, his chair coming upright in a second as he took in her too-pale face and her look of utter helplessness.

By the time he got to her she was trembling, the receiver hanging in her limp hand. Her softly uttered "Oh God" and the emotion behind it almost broke his heart.

He caught the receiver as it slipped from her hands. She walked to the couch and sank onto it, her head in her hands. He followed her, going down on one knee before her, stroking her hair back from her face.

"Lucy, what is it? What's wrong?"

When she looked up at him he saw a look in her eyes so desolate and yet so frightened that he knew he was seeing a side of this woman she had kept hidden until now.

"That was Gray," she said. "My father's been admitted to hospital. Critical-care unit. He...he had a heart attack and they aren't sure if he'll..." Live or die. Gray's words echoed in her head but she couldn't speak them. Live or die, she thought. All these years she had tried to respect her parents' wishes, had stayed away, and now in seconds, she felt the need to be with them. Her father was just a man...as vulnerable to death as anyone.

"I haven't seen him in four years."

Clayton sat down beside her. "It's never too late."

"I did a terrible thing. I tore my family apart." She

looked across at him, her eyes lifeless. "What if he doesn't want to see me...even now?"

He reached out and drew her against him, holding her. What had she done to have been banished from her family? What kind of parents could do that to a child? A parents' love was meant to be unconditional. Lucy had carried this burden with her for too long. Maybe now she would be able to face it, to resolve what was wrong with her family.

"Do you want to go?"

She nodded, taking a calming breath. "I have to. Even if he tells me to leave, I have to see him."

"Then I'm taking you down to the city," he said, not surprised when she looked at him uncertainly. "I mean it. That old heap of junk you drive won't make it. We'll take the truck."

She grasped his hand and held it tight. "It won't be pleasant, no matter what happens," she told him. "I don't want you getting caught in the cross fire."

He managed a smile. "I know when to keep my head down, darlin'. I'll give you all the privacy you want but I'm taking you there." When she would have objected he raised their hands and brushed a kiss over her knuckles. "Let me do this for you. Let somebody do something to make your life easier for once."

A shiver snaked its way down her spine. "I don't deserve to have things easy," she said cryptically, pushing to her feet as she ran her hands down her skirt. "I don't know how long I'll be there. I have to pack some things and...then there's the kids."

"Shay won't mind coming over to stay with them."

Lucy knew the other woman would be glad to help. She raised her eyes to his, wanting to take refuge in the strength she saw. "I have to go."

"I understand."

Just in case, she thought. Just in case she never got to talk to her father again, never got to hear his voice, even if all she heard was anger and sadness.

Clayton looked at his watch. "I'm going to head home and grab an overnight bag," he said, standing, grasping her shoulders in his hands, turning her to face him. "I'll bring Shay back and let Zach and Josh know what's going on. And if you try to leave without me I'll follow you, so save us both the extra worry and wait for me."

Lucy knew when to give in…not that she did it very often. And only with him, she realized with sudden insight. "All right. I'll be waiting." She hugged herself, trying to ward off the nerves starting to churn in her stomach. "It's been so long. What do I say to them?"

Four years. Clayton reached out and cupped her chin, wanting to see the fire back in her eyes, instead of this dull sadness, wanting to see that determined glint he'd gotten used to. "How about you just say g'day and see where it goes from there."

It took him twenty minutes to go home, inform his brothers, pack a bag and collect Shay. All he wanted to do was get back to Lucy…to touch her…to be near her. Lucy's pain was his pain. When she smiled he felt as if he could move mountains. Her kisses touched his soul. When he looked into her eyes he felt as if he could reach out and find heaven in their beauty…in her.

When he pulled up to Lucy's front door Shay grabbed her bag, but Clayton took it from her as he followed her inside. The kids were awake and the concern on their faces was real.

"I'm ready when you are, McKinley."

All heads turned toward the stairs and Clayton could hardly believe that this polished, sophisticated woman was his Lucy. Gone was the casual attire he was used to seeing her in. Now she wore black tailored trousers, a white blouse and a black blazer. He realized with a jolt that, from the delicate French braid in her hair to the shiny black pumps on her feet, she came from an entirely different world to him. She might not live in that world now but it was obvious she could assume her place in it just the same.

Shay hugged her. "I'll pray for your dad."

Lucy nodded. "Thank you…and again for staying here."

"I'm happy to do it. Don't worry about a thing except getting to see your dad."

One by one the kids said their goodbyes. Lisa whispered something to her. Thomas placed a comforting hand on her shoulder and Max hugged her shyly. Katie threw her arms around Lucy and held her tightly. "Come back to us, okay?"

Lucy framed the girl's face in her hands. "I will always come back," she said softly. Then she looked at each of the others. "To all of you."

Clayton picked up the small suitcase that sat near the door. "We'd better go."

Lucy followed him out the door. He settled her in the truck, placing the case with his duffel bag behind the seat before climbing in behind the wheel.

"I almost didn't recognize you," he said, starting the engine and pulling out of the yard.

She bit her lip, wondering if her explanation would sound crazy to him. "I can't be the Lucy you know, not when I'm with them. They expect more."

Clayton couldn't help it. He reached out and clasped

her hand, bringing it to rest on his thigh. "I think they would be lucky to know the Lucy I know," he said quietly, wondering why they would find his Lucy less than perfect. "What's this other Lucy like then?" When she looked across at him uncertainly, he smiled. "Just so I know what to expect."

She looked down at their joined hands. "She might get distant. And she sometimes closes herself off from everyone…it's easier that way. You'll discover things about her you don't like."

This other Lucy sounded like a facade she'd created for herself. But why would she need one? "So you have a past. We all do. Some are a little tougher to leave behind than others," he told her, rubbing his thumb back and forth over the tender skin of her hand. "Whatever you did, Lucy, you deserve their forgiveness."

She looked up at him. The pain inside her unfurled and threatened to burst in her chest. How much stress had Megan's death put on her father to precipitate a heart attack in such a healthy man? "I can't even forgive myself, McKinley. Their pain is one hundred times worse."

Clayton knew the conversation had come to an end. She sat with her back ramrod straight, the hand he wasn't holding had a white-knuckled grip on the armrest of the door and she stared aimlessly out the window at the night.

The road stretched out before him, illuminated by the truck lights. He'd heard the pain in her voice, the self-loathing. He'd only known her a short time but Clayton felt he was a good judge of character and Lucy didn't have a malicious bone in her body. He couldn't imagine what she thought was so unforgivable.

"Are you cold, darlin'?"

"No." At least not in the way he meant. Inside she was iced over. No amount of warmth would help her.

When he put the radio on she felt the loss of his touch but relieved that she wouldn't have to make conversation just now. It was still dark when they pulled into an all-night café and grabbed a quick bite and some strong hot coffee.

Lucy tried to eat the bacon and eggs he'd ordered for her but her stomach churned with all that was ahead of her and she barely managed the coffee. At some point she dozed and when she awakened dawn was on the horizon and they were almost into the city.

Clayton glanced across at her as she stirred and yawned, sitting up a little straighter in the seat. He took in the drawn, too-pale face and the unmistakable exhaustion that was as much mental as it was physical.

"Hey there, sleeping beauty," he said with a grin, braking for a traffic light.

Lucy brushed wisps of hair back from her face and took in the familiar sights and sounds of a bustling city on the verge of erupting into frenzied activity. "If I look as bad as I feel, McKinley, then the blarney is working overtime." She frowned at him. "Do you know where you're going?"

He held up the napkin she'd given him at the café. "Your directions are easier to follow than a road map."

While Clayton manoeuvred his way expertly through traffic, Lucy tried to prepare herself for what was ahead. At some point she would have to tell him about Megan. What his reaction would be she couldn't say. He had said she deserved forgiveness but he didn't know that her rebellion had cost her sister's life. Would that change the way he felt about her? she wondered. When he pulled the truck into the underground carpark at the hospital she felt sick.

He parked and got out, walking around to her side and helping her down. Then he stretched his muscles and yawned.

"You should have let me drive some of the way," she said, wondering how long it would be before he would succumb to fatigue. He was almost dead on his feet. "You worked all day yesterday. Then we went out last night and—"

He cupped her chin and lifted her gaze to his. "You needed rest," he said. "I'm used to going without sleep and if I'd felt too tired I would have pulled over or let you take the wheel. I don't play around with my life or anyone else's, Lucy." His thumb caressed her jaw. "You feel up to this?"

Lucy nodded, reaching up to brush a lock of hair back from his forehead and lost herself in those honest, blue eyes. She had never known a man so generous and giving, not only of his time but of himself. His sincerity and his sense of right and wrong were things she had never thought to find in a man...ever. And now she had. Lucy wanted to believe that he would still see her the same way when he found out what she'd done. But she didn't dare.

"Kiss me."

Chapter Nine

Clayton heard the fear, the plea. He also saw lingering desire in her eyes mingling with uncertainty. "Which Lucy would I be kissing?"

"Does it matter?"

"Yeah, it matters," he said, studying her. "I don't want the Lucy I know to disappear completely the minute you walk into that room upstairs. I need to know that when I touch you, when I kiss you, part of the Lucy you are with me will still be in there," he told her, placing the palm of his hand on her chest, feeling the beat of her heart.

Lucy covered his hand with hers, moulding it to her. "She'll be here. As long as you're waiting she won't be far away."

Clayton nodded. "Good. Now that it's settled," he said, stepping close enough that she could smell the lingering scent of aftershave, could feel the warmth of his big body. His hand slid up to her neck, his fingers in her hair. His head dipped and the first touch of his mouth was so soft she might have imagined it, but then his lips were nuzzling hers apart, teasing and coaxing until she complied out of sheer need. He didn't deepen the kiss but tasted her briefly before pulling back slightly, his breathing thready.

"I'd love to continue this, Lucy, but it's probably best that you don't go in to see your father looking well and truly ravished."

She smiled at him, knowing if it wasn't love she was feeling it was as close as she had ever been to it. "I'm glad you're here, Clayton."

"So that's what I had to do to hear you say my name," he teased. "I like the way it sounds on your lips," he said, pulling her to him.

"Seems fair," she replied, her heart in her throat. "I...I like being in your arms."

She could spend a lifetime there if she wanted to, Clayton thought. Unfortunately now was not the time to broach that subject...but he would and soon. "You ready to go up?"

She nodded, smoothing a hand over her hair, straightening her blazer. She took the arm he held out for her. "As ready as I'll ever be."

Lucy hated hospitals. The fact that this was one of the most expensive private hospitals in the state made no difference to her. The smells were the same, the clinical apparatus, the sounds of suffering. She remembered the weeks she'd spent in a place like this, unable to attend her sister's funeral. Feeling on that day as if she was alone in the world and realizing afterward that for all practical purposes, she was.

"What room number?" asked Clayton, bringing her back to the present.

She told him and they found it easily. When he would

have pushed it open she stopped him, staring blankly at it, her heart galloping, her pulse racing. She took a deep breath, squared her shoulders and, feeling as if this was the hardest thing she had ever had to do, she pushed the door open, her hand now held in his firm grip.

Clayton should probably have offered to wait out in the hall. He didn't want to intrude. But the way she was holding on to him he wasn't going anywhere but where she was.

The first thing he noticed was the pale, sleeping man in the bed, an oxygen mask over his nose and mouth. Monitors kept a silent mechanical vigil on one side of him, and wires were hooked up to the plastic patches on his chest. The woman sitting beside the bed looked like an older version of Lucy. Her dress was black, her jewellery looked like the real thing and she sat stiffly in the chair.

"Hello, Mother."

The older woman's eyes narrowed and her lips formed a thin line. "Lucille."

Lucy balked a little, not having been called that in so long. She glanced toward her father. "How is he? Do the doctors know anything yet?"

"He's improving steadily," she said, her tone icy. "You didn't have to come. I should have realized Gray would call you."

Clayton couldn't believe the callous words but they seemed to bounce off Lucy. He saw acceptance in her expression, resignation. He didn't like it one damn bit. "Lucy was frantic with worry, Mrs. Warner."

Daphne regarded him coolly. "And you would be?"

"Clayton McKinley."

Her eyes shot back to Lucy, dismissing him. "If your presence upsets your father you will leave," she told

Lucy. "I won't let your selfishness kill him. I've lost too much of my family already."

Lucy felt familiar pain, and stinging guilt. If her mother's words hadn't cut her to the quick the cold tone would have. "Regardless of the past, Father is my main concern now."

She pinned Lucy with a glacial look. "Your father or his money?"

"I'm not here for money, Mother. I neither want nor need anything from you." *Except forgiveness,* she thought. *Except love.*

A nurse came through the door then, checking monitors and tubes, making notes on the clipboard that hung on the end of the bed. She greeted Lucy, introducing herself as Nancy.

Clayton stood there glaring at Daphne. It didn't matter that she wasn't looking. It made him feel better. Only the fact that her husband lay ill in the bed had saved her from his angry words. How dare she accuse Lucy of being mercenary. He had a feeling he knew Lucy better after two weeks than this woman did after twenty-five years. Just let her try to lay that garbage on Lucy outside this room, he thought.

As the door closed behind Nancy, Elliot Warner's eyelids fluttered. His hand moved on the bed, his fingers flexing into the sheet. Lucy rushed to his side and reached down, placing her hand lightly on his. "Father?"

When his eyes opened, Lucy felt a rush of relief such as she had never known. His eyes focused on her and he reached up in haste to tear the mask from his face, over his wife's protestations.

"You...came." He coughed weakly. "So much... pain. Time...it doesn't heal."

Lucy bit down hard on her lip. "I had to come when I found out, Father, but if you want me to leave, I will."

His coughing returned with a vengeance and she reached for the mask, placing it over his face. After a few minutes he pulled it down, taking a taxing breath. "Makes no difference. Still pain...the lost years with...my daughter."

Lucy blinked back tears. Those years with Megan had been lost to him because of her. He hadn't forgotten or forgiven, but then she hadn't really expected it. It took a few minutes for his breathing to steady and Clayton found he had more questions than answers. He looked at Lucy then. She held herself as stiff as a board, her fists clenched by her sides. But it was her face that got to him, drawn into a cool blank mask. God, he wanted his sassy, amber-eyed beauty back.

Daphne rose from the chair, briefly kissing her husband's cheek before straightening. She looked at Lucy. "It caused him pain to see you here."

Lucy didn't even flinch at the words. "Gray thought I should know...and he was right."

Daphne's sigh was pure irritation. "I'd prefer you didn't come to the house."

Clayton wondered if Daphne was taking pleasure in punishing Lucy this way. It was all he could do not to tear strips off her.

"I wasn't planning to," Lucy replied. "But I'll be here until I know he's going to be all right."

Clayton touched her shoulder. "Do you want to stay until your father wakes again?"

"That would be pointless," said Daphne. "He needs his rest."

Lucy's eyes never left her father. "I'll check with the nurse."

Daphne shot her a dark look and walked to the door, pausing on the threshold. "I don't want you here, Lucille. You stir bad memories. You always will."

Clayton could no longer remain silent, not even for Lucy. "It's been four years," he said impatiently. "Hasn't Lucy done her penance?"

Daphne glared at him, her expression showing the first signs of real emotion as tears pooled in her eyes. "Tell me, Mr. McKinley, what should the penance be for someone who killed her own sister?"

Clayton looked at Lucy. She stood silent, her expression cold and distant.

"You didn't know?" Daphne asked, her gaze piercing. "Ask her about Megan, about the night she died. Then you can talk to me about penance."

The door whooshed closed behind her. Lucy bent to kiss her father's forehead then she straightened the sheet at his chest. "Gray's meeting will keep him interstate until tomorrow, but he told me on the phone he's had rooms prepared at his house," she said, sounding less like the Lucy he knew every minute. "We need to talk."

Clayton was about to tell her the same thing. If this was what she'd had to deal with in her past, it was no wonder she withdrew into herself to handle it. He turned her to face him, waiting patiently until she got curious and looked up at him. "I wish things could have been different for you."

"I've been wishing that for so long now."

He reached for her but she pulled away. "Don't judge her too harshly, Clayton. When you hear the whole story you'll see she's justified."

"I won't ever believe she has a right to treat you like that," he said, brushing a kiss against her forehead. "It doesn't matter what you tell me.'' But he could see she was far from convinced.

They found the nurses' station and Nancy smiled cheerfully as Lucy made her enquiry. ''He's stabilized. He'll more than likely sleep for most of this morning and well into the afternoon. The doctor has restricted his visitors to family. Visiting hours are from four until nine this evening so if you want to pop back then I'm sure he'll be awake.''

Lucy nodded. ''If I could leave you the number I can be reached at,'' she said, accepting the piece of paper and pen that Nancy passed to her. She scribbled Gray's number and handed it to the other woman. ''Please call if anything...''

Nancy nodded. ''Of course I will, but you have to keep a positive outlook,'' she said as a buzzer went off behind her. She excused herself and hurried down the hall.

''Seems like he's in good hands,'' said Clayton, putting an arm around her shoulder, not surprised when he felt her stiffen. But at least she didn't pull away.

''Let's get out of here,'' she said, walking to the bank of elevators. ''You need to get some sleep.''

He wasn't about to argue with her that he wasn't tired. He felt as exhausted as she looked. ''Gray Harrison's been a good friend to you, hasn't he, Lucy?''

She managed a smile that reached her eyes and took a deep breath as they stepped into the elevator. ''He saved my life at a time when I didn't want to live anymore. I love him more than I can say.''

Her words sliced through him. He'd wondered from the very first night they had met just how deeply she felt for Gray. Now he didn't need to wonder. The love in her voice when she spoke of him told Clayton that her feelings for the other man went deep. She had emotions for Gray that Clayton could never compete with. He'd never cared enough to be jealous before about any woman and he sure as hell didn't like the feeling. Yet with Lucy it was instinctive. He didn't want to analyze it, not now. But he knew he wanted the position in her heart that Gray Harrison occupied.

Lucy gave him directions to the Harrison estate and wasn't surprised that he handled the inner-city traffic with the same confidence as he did everything else. She leaned back in her seat wishing for the wide-open spaces of Cable Creek and casting a glance at him now and again, wondering why he had grown so quiet.

"I'm sorry Mother wasn't more polite to you."

He shrugged. "I'm sorry if I spoke out of turn," he replied. "I just wasn't prepared to stand there and listen to her say those things about you."

"I thought…maybe she'd come to accept things." Lucy looked out the window aimlessly. "I should have known she would never forgive me."

Minutes later they pulled into the semicircular driveway of the Harrison estate. Clayton took in the carefully manicured lawns and gardens, the three-story mansion, elegant and colonial in design. Ivy grew up the walls and ground staff pottered around, glancing up at the new arrivals.

They were met at the door by a man Lucy introduced as Harvey, who promptly shook Clayton's hand. Middle-aged and balding, he had kind eyes and a shy smile. He greeted Lucy warmly, inquiring as to how she had been. Clayton was glad someone made it clear they were pleased to see her.

"Mr. Harrison said your stay is an indefinite one," he said, leading them into the grandest entrance hall Clayton had ever seen. "I've prepared your old room and Mr. McKinley may use the one next door to it. Brunch is ready, but considering the long journey, I thought you might like to freshen up or take a nap. If you or Mr. McKinley need anything, please don't hesitate to call."

"Thank you, Harvey. I think we both need sleep before we eat," she said, casting a questioning glance at Clayton. He nodded agreement.

Harvey excused himself, leaving them alone.

"Gray's come a long way from Cable Creek," said Clayton, marveling at the size of the place. "I guess he got what he always wanted."

Lucy sighed. "Not everything," she said cryptically.

Clayton took her hand, still wondering about her comment. "Lead the way, darlin'."

They made their way up the spiral staircase. Lucy showed him the well-equipped gymnasium, the sauna and the large games room complete with a competition-size billiards table, wide-screen television and a state-of-the-art sound system. He even had an old fifties-style jukebox. "What's on the second floor?"

"Guest rooms in the east wing, Gray's rooms, including his office, are in the west wing." Lucy led him down the hall. "His office here is larger than the one in the city," she said. "He has a library, and a small cinema as well."

Clayton shook his head at the size of the mansion. "He could live quite comfortably here and never have to leave."

"I'm sure there have been times when he's considered it," she said, coming to her room. Nothing had changed, she realized, looking around the spacious room with its large four-poster bed. The curtains were the same, the carpet too. Along one wall her stuffed-animal collection sat staring down at her. Along another, shelves of her beloved books. Even the quilt on her bed, she realized, was the same one she'd had when she'd last seen this room. Of course, the room smelled clean and fresh with not a speck of dust anywhere.

"This was your room?"

Lucy looked at him in surprise. Then the tone of his voice gave away his thoughts. "Yes. You thought I shared a room with Gray, didn't you? You thought we were...lovers?"

Clayton couldn't decide whether or not she was angry at him. "Yes, I did. The way you talked about him...the look you get in your eyes when you mention his name."

"Men and women can be friends and not make love. You and I are friends."

"And if things were different, darlin', we'd be making love. You can bet your last dollar on that."

She shook her head and clasped her hands in front of her, looking up at him, her gaze direct and unwavering. "I love Gray but we were never lovers."

Clayton felt the pressure ease in the vicinity of his heart. But if they had not been lovers what had forged the bond between them, a bond he sensed was unbreakable?

"How old were you when you came to live here, Lucy?"

She walked to the window and looked out, finally glancing back at him. "Eighteen."

His jaw clenched. "Your parents kicked you out, didn't they?"

"They suggested I find other accommodation. I was off to university anyway. I had a nervous breakdown and was ordered to take a year off before starting uni."

Clayton wondered how long this anger would last. Her

parents had abandoned her, and no matter what she had done, nothing could justify that in his eyes. "Gray took you in."

She nodded. "He was five years older than me and a friend of the family since my father invested in his first venture and made them both millions of dollars," she said, her smile soft and reminiscent. "Gran left me a trust fund that I received just after I left home. It paid my way through university."

Clayton turned her toward the bed and propelled her gently forward until she sat on the edge of it. He slipped off her shoes, then helped her out of her jacket.

"Would you lie here with me until I fall asleep, Clayton?"

"Stretch out, darlin'." He kicked off his boots and shucked out of his jacket, dropping it on the end of the bed before crawling over beside her, his back against the headboard. He opened his arms to her and Lucy went because she needed to be held, to feel warmth instead of this chill she'd been carrying with her since they'd left the hospital. He pillowed her head on his broad chest, settling one hand, palm down, on his stomach, feeling the rigid muscles beneath.

"Megan was three years older than me," she began. "I...envied her because she did everything right. Straight-A student. People gravitated toward her. She was vivacious and clever and...I loved her."

Clayton tightened his arms around her as the last three words caught on a sob. And as her tears fell steadily he listened as she told him how she had gone against her parents' wishes nine years ago. About how she had sneaked out of the house to a secret rendezvous with a boy they disapproved of, once they'd gone for the evening. As she spoke he could picture her upset and confused over the disaster of her first sexual experience, afraid her parents would find out. Panicked, she'd called her sister.

"I was ashamed and sick at what I'd done. I just wanted someone to need me…and Ian said he did. But he was looking for comfort too and we thought we'd find it with each other. We were wrong."

Clayton kissed the top of her head. "Don't be ashamed of anything you've done," he told her. "Sex for the first time is rarely the ideal we think it will be."

She nestled closer. "It was awful and I cried so much because it hurt and because I knew deep down inside that it wasn't the right time, the right person. Poor Ian didn't know how to handle my reaction."

Clayton wondered what he would have done in the same situation. Granted, his first time hadn't been quite so traumatic, but nerves and inexperience could make it bad for anyone. "I wish it had been better for you."

"There hasn't ever been any other man," she told him softly. "I wish it had been you."

Clayton sucked in a breath at her statement even as his body reacted to her words and the proximity of her body. His arousal had been stirring since he'd pulled her into his arms, and though they were on a bed, she needed him in a different way. "When I make love to you, Lucy, it will be your first time as far as I'm concerned."

Lucy's heart raced at the thought of sharing that intimacy with him. The way he made her feel with just a kiss or a touch assured her it would be incredible with him.

"Megan came to pick me up," she continued. "It was pouring rain and I'd interrupted her studying but she was so concerned about me when I told her what I'd done." Lucy closed her eyes, seeing that long-ago night, hearing

MARY KATE HOLDER 155

the sounds. "She reached across and took my hand. She
said it hurt her to see my pain and that she would always
be here for me because we were sisters and...sisters
were forever. Then it happened."

She was trembling in his arms now, her breathing
choppy and erratic. "The car came from nowhere. It ran
a stop sign. We found out later that the driver was
drunk," she said, sniffling as she wiped at her tears.
"Megan tried to swerve but the car hit on her side. It
took them two hours to cut her free and she was con-
scious the whole time. I couldn't do anything to help
her. You know, I only stopped hearing her cries in my
sleep a year ago," she told him. "They stayed with me
for so long."

"I'm so sorry it happened, darlin'" he said, pulling
her as close as he could get her, tightening his arms
around her shoulders as his chin rested on the top of her
head. "Were you hurt?"

She nodded. "Not as badly as Megan," she said, dismissing the injuries that had kept her in hospital for six
weeks afterward. "She died that night on the operating
table," said Lucy, pain filling every word. She tightened
her arms around Clayton's waist. "I never got to say
goodbye."

Then the tears came, a torrent that tore at his insides.
It was as if she had stored up all her pain and misery,
all the torment she had lived with and now it was breaking free, demanding she acknowledge it. He did the only
thing he could do. He held her, wanting to share her
pain and sadness as he wanted to share the rest of her
life.

After twenty minutes her crying had subsided to the
occasional soft sob and he thought she might fall asleep
any minute. Then she stirred in his arms.

"My parents demanded to know what we'd been doing out," she said, sounding more in control of her emotions now. "I told them and my father exploded. I've never seen him so angry. My mother looked at me as if I had killed Megan with my own two hands. I had four months to complete my final year of high school and because they felt it their duty, my parents let me finish out the term living at home."

"God, it must have been hell living there," he said, knowing in his heart that their attitude to her had hardened from that night on. It explained the way her mother had been today and why Lucy hadn't seen her parents for so long. Clayton fought back the anger. Had her parents not seen that Lucy was a victim too?

"When Gray asked me to move in here I was stunned." She looked up at him. "He'd proposed to Megan one month before the accident. They were going to be married."

So Gray hadn't really changed that much from the kid he had grown up with. He had lost the woman he'd loved but he hadn't turned his back on Lucy. Clayton listened as she spoke of university, her degree, her career working with troubled street kids and how that had been Megan's dream. Gray had tried to talk her out of pursuing her sister's dream, had tried to persuade her into following her own.

"But I had none," she said, sighing with exhaustion. "When Megan died I hadn't even considered my future after school. But I'd listened to her tell me so many times what she wanted to do with her life. All I could do for her in the end was make her dream come true."

Clayton knew she had come to love the dream and not just live it. "Megan kept her promise to always be there for you even after she died, Lucy. I believe that.

But she wouldn't want you to carry the guilt about what happened."

"The guilt reminds me," she said, stifling a yawn. "It reminds me that selfishness has consequences."

In minutes her breathing was steady and even, her fingers slackening on his shirt. Her body relaxed into his and Clayton let out a deep sigh. He drifted off to sleep with Lucy in his arms, with her words echoing in his head and her pain lingering in his heart.

When he woke hours later Lucy was sitting at the table in the corner of the room. He rolled off the bed and walked over to her, placing his hands on her shoulders and his lips on her neck as his arms slipped around her. She'd showered, he realized, her hair still slightly damp and hanging down her back, her skin smelling of soap and lavender.

"You smell incredible, darlin'. If we didn't have to get back to the hospital I'd talk you back into bed...and not to sleep either." He glanced at the table. "This looks good."

Lucy's stomach clenched and she managed a smile. "Thank you for listening earlier...for not judging me."

He shot her a wry grin and sat down as she uncovered a plate before him. "Thank you for trusting me enough to tell me about Megan...about yourself."

She nodded and seemed content to let the subject go. Clayton wouldn't push. She'd had a hell of a morning already. He didn't realize how hungry he was until he viewed the aromatic, still-warm omelette. "I'll grab a shower when I finish this and we can head back to the hospital," he said, glancing at his watch.

She smiled sadly at him. "I can't believe how much I want them back in my life. For so long I've lived with just knowing they were here...close by. Now..."

Clayton took her hand, kneeling down beside her, one hand on the back of her chair. "They're your family, darlin'. As badly as they've treated you, they're—"

"They haven't treated me badly, Clayton. I took Megan away from them because of my selfishness."

He looked into her eyes, the swirling amber depths, and the realization sliced at his heart. She didn't see herself as a victim, didn't see Megan's death as an accident. In Lucy's mind she was the villain. Damn, if only her parents could see what they had done to her with their guilt.

"You didn't stop being their daughter when Megan died," he told her calmly. "She was taken from them by a drunk driver, but they gave you up as well. They didn't fight for you when they should have." And to Clayton it was just that simple. He placed a kiss on her fingers and managed a smile. "I'll go grab that shower and we can be on our way."

Lucy watched him go, seeing the weariness in his posture and his face. The look of absolute faith she saw in his eyes when he spoke to her warmed her deep inside in places that had been so cold and dark for so very long. He had gotten into her heart despite her best efforts to keep him out. He made her want all the things she had denied herself.

He hadn't spoken a word about commitment, about permanence. And yet Lucy knew if he asked her to become his lover she would say yes in a heartbeat because his tenderness and caring had begun to thaw her resolve not to get involved.

An affair wouldn't be so bad and she had no doubt the physical side of it would be like nothing she had ever experienced, the spark between them was just that hot. She could allow herself an affair with him. She craved his touch, needed him in her life for however long he wanted her in his. She couldn't give him a lifetime…her guilt would not allow it. But an affair was something she could live with. Lucy just hoped she could walk away when it was over.

Chapter Ten

When they arrived at the hospital her father's doctor met them at the nurses' station. He ushered Lucy into the nearby waiting room and Clayton followed, not budging even after a cool, dismissive look from the gray-haired man. He would leave when and if Lucy asked him to and not a minute before.

"Lucy, your father got quite upset when he woke just after lunch. It took us quite a while to calm him down. By the time I got to the room your mother was frantic."

Lucy crossed her arms in front of her and glared at the doctor. "Is he going to be all right?"

"Not if he has episodes like that again." He managed a stiff smile. "Your mother has asked that you not be allowed in to see him again."

Lucy felt as if he'd slapped her. "Ask my father how he feels about having me here."

"And risk another heart attack? Maybe worse? His prognosis is precarious at best. I have to do what I think is best for him."

Lucy nodded, not feeling anger or pain. She didn't feel anything now…just a need to go home, a need to see her kids and get back to the life she had carved for herself. "May I see him before I go?"

"He might wake up and see you there. I can't allow it." He walked down the hall, leaving them alone.

"I need to pick up some things from Gray's house," she said as if let out of a dream. "When I visit Megan we can go home."

"We can stay until your father's out of danger, Lucy."

"He has a better chance of recovery if I'm not here. I don't want him upset." She cursed softly. "I should never have come."

"I'm glad you're finally seeing reason."

They both looked up at the sound of Daphne's voice. Clayton had expected to see her gloating but instead her expression was one of sadness and pain.

"He doesn't want you here. Can't you understand what it's like for us…for me?" she asked, her voice not quite so calm now. "I see you and it reminds me that Megan is dead. I remember the wedding she was planning. I imagine the children she'll never bear and Gray losing the woman he loved." She shook her head. "I don't have his capacity for forgiveness, Lucille. I've tried but…this is the only way I know to deal with the pain."

It was the closest Lucy had ever seen her mother come to sharing her emotions, allowing people to see her pain. Such a pity, she thought, that it was too late. "I lost her too, Mother. Megan was my sister and I loved her."

"You went out to be with that boy and your sister lost her life because of it."

"And because of one mistake she pays for the rest of

her life?'' Clayton asked, meeting Daphne's glare head-on. "Did you ever stop to think that maybe the accident had something to do with a drunk driver who had no right being on the road?''

Daphne glared at him before looking back to her daughter. "You're living Megan's dreams," she said coldly. "But they will never mean as much to you as they did to her. You can have love and marriage, probably even children someday, but you'll have it at your sister's expense. Go home. Live your life. And pray you never know the pain of burying a child. It's a pain that shows no mercy. May your guilt keep you company as my heartache has done to me.''

As her mother walked away, Clayton cupped Lucy's chin and made her meet his eyes. "She had no right to say any of those things to you.''

"Yes, she did. And every word was true.'' A single tear rolled over her cheek but she didn't reach up to brush it away. "Everything I've got, everything I...thought I could have is more than I deserve.''

Clayton felt sick inside, knowing she'd included him in that "everything." "Lucy, bad things happen. If we'd badgered my mother to see the doctor when she started getting tired all the time I might still have both my parents. You can't live your life with blame and guilt stalking you. That isn't living...it's existing.'' But he could see his words made no impact on her pain.

"Let's go,'' she said quietly, wiping her cheeks with trembling fingers. "If we get lucky with the traffic we might even make it home before it gets too late.''

Clayton followed her to the elevators and down to the car park in silence. Before they headed out, Lucy asked to make a stop.

At the cemetery, Clayton watched her fingers smooth

over the writing on the nameplate. He stood off to the side, hands in his pockets. Lucy would always feel guilty for Megan. The death of her sister wasn't Lucy's penance, he thought. Nor was losing contact with her parents. Living was Lucy's penance. Living with the guilt and the pain.

Back at the house Lucy loaded the things from her room into storage boxes she found in Gray's attic. There she also found a box that had come from her parents a few weeks after she'd left. Lucy had never had the heart to go through it. Maybe in time she would. Memories were all she had now. She said goodbye to Harvey and left Gray a note that Harvey assured her he would receive the minute he returned.

She willed herself to sleep all the way home and even when she woke halfway through the journey, she kept her eyes closed, pretending she was. It was the coward's way out but it wasn't as though she hadn't traveled that road before. When they pulled into the yard hours later, the house was dark.

"Looks like everyone's in bed," she said, secretly pleased she wouldn't have to face the kids tonight. She would handle their questions in the morning. "I didn't think to call and tell Shay I'd be back tonight."

"If she's asleep just get Thomas to bring her home in the morning or one of us can come and get her."

Lucy nodded, drowning in the awful silence that followed. When she found her courage the words came. "I can't see you anymore," she said, averting her eyes. "Except as neighbours. I'd like it if you kept up your friendship with the kids though. They need strong role models in their lives and your family is about the best I know of."

Clayton had expected things to be tough, especially after what her mother had said to her, because Lucy believed it, truly believed that she had gained by her sister's death. But he hadn't expected her to send him away and he hadn't counted on it hurting so damn much.

"I'm not letting you go."

Lucy felt like crying all over again. She'd cried more today than she had in the last nine years.

"Please don't say that," she pleaded, her eyes suspiciously moist.

"Why, Lucy? Because you think you're not worthy of someone wanting you in their life? You think you don't deserve to be cared for and protected? Your mother spoke out of anger and hurt. And she was wrong."

She stared out the window at the full moon that illuminated everything with a pearly-white sheen, but he grasped her chin and turned her face to his, staring into her eyes as though he could see through to her soul.

"You are the first man in my life since Ian," she said quietly. "After nine years of not letting anyone get close to me, you managed to do it in less than two weeks."

He looked away, his jaw clenched, a muscle ticking there. Lucy didn't want to say any more but he needed to hear it. She had to make him see. "What you made me feel was a gift, Clayton. You made me feel special and I haven't had that in so long." His gaze shot back to her then and he reached out to take her hand in a grip she probably could have pulled away from.

"I can't explain what I'm feeling," he said honestly. "But I know in my heart it's real and when you're in my arms I know you feel it too. Maybe not love, but something worth taking a shot at."

"You want what your parents had," she reminded

him. "I can't think about having that kind of happiness for myself without seeing Megan's body trapped in that car." And how can I forgive myself, she thought, when my parents can't bear to look at me...can't forgive me.

"I fooled myself believing I could forget. I started thinking about the future without dread in my heart," she told him. "But today I came face-to-face with the pain and suffering I caused my parents. It's been nine years and my mother still can't bear to be near me." She took a deep breath and brushed at a tear on her cheek. "I can't escape Megan's death or my part in it. And I won't let you squander your emotions on me."

For almost the first time in his life Clayton McKinley was facing a situation that he couldn't just make right through sheer stubbornness and dogged perseverance. He reached out to tuck a strand of hair behind her ear. "Then I guess it's time you asked yourself how much you love your sister."

Her surprise was the reaction he'd expected. "You know how much I love Megan."

"Do you love her enough to face your demons and set yourself free?" he asked, hating the pain he saw in her eyes and damning himself for putting it there. "Do you love Megan enough to stop living for her and start living because of her?"

Lucy swallowed the hurt his words caused her. How could he say something like that to her. "Do you think I like feeling this way? Living with the guilt?"

Clayton shook his head. "No, but I think it makes you feel safe." She opened her mouth to object but he put his fingers on her lips and stalled her. "The guilt insulates you from life, Lucy. It gives you a reason not to take risks."

Lucy began to tremble. His words were coming too

close to home…they were making too much sense and she didn't want to hear it. "The guilt reminds me—"

"That you made a mistake? That you did something reckless and stupid? We all do, Lucy."

"You didn't kill anyone," she said, her voice cold, her eyes cutting into him with their bleakness.

"Neither did you, but it's easier to think you did, isn't it?"

Lucy couldn't stop the fresh tears that slid down her cheeks. "Why are you being so cruel?"

Clayton felt his heart break at her words. He wiped her tears with the tips of his fingers, marveling at how soft her skin was, how her mouth parted slightly on a quiet sigh, her eyes fixed on him. "I wouldn't hurt you for the world, Lucy, and I think deep down inside you know it."

With that he dipped his head and touched his lips to hers. He parted her lips with his tongue and tasted her once, twice…and one last time before he brushed a kiss to her forehead and pulled away.

"Your guilt is keeping you safe for now, safe from life, from having to take chances like the rest of us," he told her, prepared for the hurt he saw in her eyes. "But eventually it will suffocate you, Lucy. I won't watch you destroy yourself over something that was an accident."

He opened his door and got out, unloading the box from the back of the truck. Lucy unlocked the front door and he deposited it on the living-room floor.

She wanted to say so much to him, to tell him that the guilt had become her best friend, her constant companion. Lucy wanted to tell him she was falling in love with him. She'd realized it lying in his arms, telling him about Megan and the night she died. Against her better judgement and despite her best efforts she had fallen in love with Clayton McKinley.

He closed the cover on the back of the truck and secured it before walking slowly toward her. He stopped inches from where she stood. "I'll be seeing you."

Lucy shook her head, unable to look at him. "That wouldn't be a good idea. We need to make this a clean break, Clayton."

"We're still friends, Lucy, and you want me," he said with certainty. "Just as much as I want you." If he was leaving, he'd give her something to think about. "I couldn't go a day now without seeing you, without hearing you." He searched her face. "Without touching you."

Lucy choked back the tears that threatened. "You've already given me so much more than I thought I would ever have. You've made me feel things for the first time in years…and I thank you for that."

With that she turned and walked inside, closing the door behind her. She didn't need anyone else's forgiveness, he realized. She needed to forgive herself and that would be a choice Lucy would have to make.

For the next few days Lucy worked herself from dawn until dusk every single day to keep him out of her mind, to stop herself from dwelling on what a coward she was and what she had given up. Nothing worked.

It was a Friday afternoon when Lucy found herself completely alone. Max and Katie were at school, Lisa had gone shopping with Caroline for something to wear to an upcoming town social, Thomas had gone with Zach to a stock sale in Guthrie and Shay was working a double shift at the Roadhouse.

There were no more excuses she could use to put off going through the box that had sat in the corner of the lounge room since she'd returned from Sydney. She knelt down, lifting the lid and began searching through it.

In this box was her childhood. A favourite doll and a jigsaw puzzle she'd made at school. Drawings, paintings and birthday cards. Stickers and stamps and colouring books. And journals...eight of them, a chronicle of her teenage years filled with words and thoughts and the hopes she'd had before Megan's death. She sat down on the floor and began leafing through one of them, shaking her head at the arrogance of youth, reading how she'd viewed the world as a rebellious fourteen-year-old.

As she lifted the last journal from the box she stilled, a rush of cool air suddenly coming from nowhere and raising goose bumps on her skin even as it gave her a sense of peace. But her eyes never strayed from the leather-bound book on the bottom of the box. She didn't need to open it and read the words inside. She didn't wonder how it had ended up in this box meant for her, instead of in Megan's room at her parents' house or with Gray.

With a hand that trembled she lifted Megan's journal out of the box. The moment she touched it she felt a warm presence nearby, a calming one that didn't frighten her. It compelled her to read what was inside. She turned each page, realizing by the dates that this was the journal Megan had started the year she'd died. Lucy devoured each word, too grateful to question why she was given this connection with her sister again after missing her for so long. And then she came to an entry made the night Gray had proposed to her.

Dear Diary,

Gray wants me to be his wife and I've accepted. I just know Mother will want me to wear a dress that will make me look like a giant meringue, like Heather's mother did last year, but what I wear isn't as important as who I'm marrying. I love him so much that for the first time in my life I am lost for words to share with you. Lucy seems a little sad though. She's been troubled lately. Each time I try to talk to her she just smiles and tells me she's fine. She's drifting, trying to find her place in the world. She charges ahead in life without fear, not procrastinating over silly things like most of us...like me. She's headstrong and outspoken even when she knows others will disapprove.

I wish I had her strength, her ability to meet life head-on and make every second count. I hope she never loses that. She might not know where she's going but I know for her it will be an amazing journey. She has taught me so much and I hope I've done at least that much for her. Mother and Father love her but Lucy doesn't see it. She battles them at every turn and if she could realize how much she means to them I think it would make all the difference to them and to Lucy.

As for me? Well, Diary, life is for the living. Nothing is certain, nothing is promised to us and nothing is forever...except what we hold in our hearts today.

P.S. My sister told me that.

Lucy reached up to wipe away the tears that rolled down her face. She looked around expecting to see Megan standing there, so powerful had been her presence for just a few minutes. She'd never really believed in fate, in things being meant to happen. And her faith had taken a battering after the accident, but this journal had sat in a dusty attic for nine years, waiting for her to find it. Why now? she wondered. After all, it was just a journal, not some ancient book with mystical powers.

And yet Lucy couldn't shake the feeling that she had been destined to find it now…at this moment in her life. Had she battled her parents for nothing? Had they loved her even though they couldn't show it? And Megan had been envious of her when all the while Lucy had wanted to be more like her!

Lucy didn't feel strong, and instead of meeting life now she turned away from it when it really mattered. After the accident, she'd given up the journey Megan had written about, but she would never be sorry about the one she had taken instead. That thought chilled her.

Lucy closed the book and hugged it to her, realizing that she had let go, to make peace with her own conscience. It was long overdue. With trembling fingers she dialed Gray's office number and prayed he was in. She would need his help to do this…to put things right and move on with her life.

Lucy arrived at her destination the next afternoon. The hospital looked as foreboding as it had the first time she'd come. Gray had promised her he would get her parents to agree to a meeting. Even the doctor had sanctioned it. How Gray had done it she didn't know and she didn't care. The important thing was that she was here. It was a start.

Lucy thought of the kids back home, and how Shay had jumped at the chance to stay with them again, of how Josh had loaned her a reliable farm vehicle for the journey. She had made wonderful friends in Cable Creek.

She opened the door to the private room. Her father rested in the bed, his colour slightly better than last time she had seen him. Her mother stood beside him, tension practically radiating from her.

Gray held out his hand to her and led her farther into the room, an approving smile on his face that encouraged her when she felt like running. She turned back to her parents and didn't notice when he slipped quietly out the door, closing it softly behind him.

"Mum, Dad. We need to talk." Her voice was crisp and determined even as she clenched Megan's journal in front of her. "It's time."

Elliot took his wife's hand and nodded. "Yes it is."

Clayton stacked another bale of hay and wiped the sweat from his face with his shirt before hanging it on a nearby rail. Forty bales down, ten to go and he was relishing the burn of his muscles, the searing in his lungs and he was looking forward to the ache he would suffer tomorrow. He was used to physical work but he also knew his limits and he'd passed them about an hour ago when he'd gotten thrown for the fifth time from the horse Zach had vowed couldn't be rode.

Clayton had almost broken every bone in his body proving his brother wrong. He'd tried everything these past few days to get her out of his mind. Work. Traveling to stock sales. Even alcohol—but she'd been back in his mind before the hangover had even worn off. His brothers had asked him about it and he'd given them the succinct answer that he was handling it. Then he'd gotten drunk and told them everything. The kids had kept him company. They chatted about Lucy, about mundane things that she did each day and Clayton devoured the details like a starving man.

This morning they had been full of the news of Lucy's return from the city and of Gray's arrival. They'd said how excited Lucy was, how much happier she seemed now. Clayton didn't even try to kid himself about what he was feeling this time. It was jealousy. Pure unadulterated, green-eyed jealousy. He knew that the other man had met her in Sydney. And something had happened that had changed her. Even Shay had commented on how content Lucy seemed now. But the thought of the other man over there at Lucy's house, putting things right for her, making her feel safe. It ate away at him.

He looked at the stack of hay still to be moved and cursed. He'd come to the end of his patience. She could push him away, she could order him off her property if she wanted, but damn it all, he was going back over there and he would make her listen. If she threw him out he would haunt her every minute of every day until she gave him…gave them…a chance. And fifty bales of hay would, he figured, work out all his frustration and allow him to confront her with a clear head.

"Zach said I might find you here."

Clayton spun around at the sound of a voice he hadn't heard for many years. Gray Harrison was a little older but other than that he hadn't changed. With coal-black hair cut conservatively short and wearing tailored trousers and a crisp white shirt, even out here in rural Australia he exuded an air of wealth and unbreakable determination. He stood a little over six feet and had retained the athletic physique that had made him a champion at high school football.

With age had come a hardening, not just of that physique but a hardness that showed in his eyes. They were still shuttered, still keeping the world at bay. This was the man who had loved and lost the woman he'd planned to marry. Clayton thought of living a day without Lucy in his life and it almost tore out his heart. Clayton would hazard a guess that Gray had hardened to survive the pain of losing Megan. And who could blame him?

"It's been a long time."

Gray nodded, casting an eye at the bales of hay. "You won't be any use to her if you work yourself to death."

Clayton glared at him. "You should know there's always chores to do on a farm. This has nothing to do with Lucy."

Gray shook his head. "She tenses up at the mere mention of your name and you're attacking these bales of hay like you're possessed. You need to talk to her."

"Oh, I intend to," he said, promise in his tone, determination in his heart. "And this time she'll listen to me if I have to tie her to the damn chair."

Gray was silent for so long that Clayton finally dropped the bale of hay at his feet and looked up. "What are your intentions toward Lucy?"

Clayton would have laughed had he not seen the serious look in Gray's eyes. Though some dregs of jealousy lingered inside him, most of them were blown away by that simple statement. This man cared about Lucy and Clayton couldn't fault him for that.

"Isn't this a conversation I'm supposed to be having with her father?"

Gray smiled slowly. "That can be arranged. He'll be coming to visit when he's well enough."

"So they've talked?"

Gray nodded.

"Good. Lucy needs them in her life."

"On that we agree," Gray replied, stuffing his hands in his trouser pockets. "Care to answer my question?"

Clayton wedged the baling hook in the hay and took off his gloves, meeting Gray's direct look with one of his own. "No, I don't think I will. Lucy knows how I feel about her."

"Does she?"

Clayton scowled. "Meaning?"

"Women have always come easily to you, Clayton. Even when we were teenagers they were drawn to you. Now, I know your father raised you to respect women, but this is Lucy and she's damn important to me."

Clayton could have told Gray that Lucy was damn important to him too. "She's important to a lot of people. Those kids she loves as if they were her own. My family." After a pause he added, "Me."

Gray's eyes held warning. "Don't screw with her life, and then bail when the going gets rough."

Clayton had come to the end of his rope. He stepped over the bale of hay at his feet and stalked toward Gray. "I don't screw with people's lives," he said, his tone all challenge and tension. "I don't walk away from things that mean the most to me and I won't ever bail on the woman I love."

"You love me?"

Chapter Eleven

Both men turned at the sound of Lucy's voice. Gray cleared his throat. Clayton just stared, the urge to beat Gray senseless draining out of him. He hadn't even admitted it to himself until he'd said the words aloud. He'd thought a lot about what he wanted from her these past few days. He wanted a lifetime of holding her in his arms as she slept. He wanted years of seeing her smile, of hearing her sassy comebacks. He wanted her heart and her soul and every day he could spend with her. God in heaven, he *was* in love with her.

"Ah, if you'll excuse me I think I'll go up to the house and say hello to the kids," said Gray.

Lucy dragged her eyes from Clayton, still trying to come to terms with what he'd just said. She turned to Gray. She held the journal in her hands and now she passed it to him. He took it, taking a deep breath as he read Megan's name embossed in gold lettering on the cover. His fingers moved lovingly, tenderly over the leather and for a moment he smiled.

"Your friendship to me has been more than I deserved, Gray, and I can never repay all you've done for me, all you've given me. You forced me to pick up the pieces after Megan died and get on with life...and you led by example even though it was hard for you to see me each day, to know I'd survived and she had died."

"She loved you, Lucy," he said, his strong, resonant voice quieter than she'd ever heard it.

Lucy nodded. "She loved you too, Gray. She always will, wherever she is."

Clayton watched as Gray engulfed Lucy in a hug. Seeing them together, hearing them talk, he knew now how deep their love went and how special it was.

Lucy smiled up at him as he drew back. "She would want you to be happy, Gray."

He studied the journal in his hands for a long moment. "I've had happiness, Lucy. Some people only ever find it once in their lives." He squeezed Lucy's hand and nodded to Clayton as he turned and walked away.

Alone with her now Clayton couldn't believe Lucy was actually here. It occurred to him then that she was wearing a dress, pale blue in colour with short sleeves and a skirt that billowed around her calves. The bodice hugged her curves and reminded him of how it felt to have her in his arms. Her hair was down, softly framing her face, and she smiled tentatively.

He reached for his shirt and shrugged into it, not bothering to button it. He knew what he looked like, sweaty and dusty and probably mean as hell. His jeans were the oldest, rattiest pair he owned and he had a two-day growth that no doubt made him look like a derelict, but he didn't care.

"Gray said you spoke with your parents?"

She let out a breath. "Yes. It was time."

"Time for what?"

"To put the past in its place, to stop being a coward." She could see he was about to object to her words and she held up a hand to stall him, trying to ignore how potently masculine he looked, his smooth chest exposed by the open shirt, a slight sheen of sweat on his body.

"It's true and we both know it. That day in the hospital, my father wanted to talk…about me, about putting things right. He wasn't angry with me…but I jumped to conclusions."

Clayton heard the wonder in her voice, but he also heard the serenity. "And your mother?"

"She's…dealing with things. We will never be close again but maybe in time she'll be able to look at me and feel something other than sadness."

"I'm happy for you," he said. "They'll be proud of the woman you are and what you've achieved."

Lucy shrugged. "Time will tell."

She sat down on the nearest bale of hay, her hands clenched in her lap, her eyes fixed on his. She looked…different today but it wasn't the dress or the hairstyle, it was something more, something deeper. He didn't want to spook her, to make her angry with him and see her storm off but… Ah, hell! He might as well just say it.

"I was working my way through these bales before coming over to see you." She looked up at him, wide-eyed and silent. "I'm in love with you, Lucy, so you're just going to have to get used to it."

She didn't say a word, just studied him with wide eyes and a calm expression that was driving him nuts. He charged ahead while he had the chance. "I don't expect you to feel the same…not just yet. If you ever tell me you love me I want it to be because you believe the words, because you feel them in your heart.''

Clayton was prepared for her objections and denials, for her anger, even for her to argue with him until sundown. What he wasn't prepared for was the soft smile or the peace he sensed in her.

''I owe you an apology.''

All his well-rehearsed speeches were forgotten as her words knocked the wind from his lungs. ''I think I'm going to sit down for this one.'' He plonked down on a hay bale, his eyes never leaving her. He saw her slight hesitation and the way she forced herself to hold his gaze.

''I was using Megan's death as an excuse, and I finally realized why. The accident, Megan's death, made me afraid for the first time in my life. Suddenly there were things I saw I couldn't control and it was easier to wear the blame for the accident and its aftermath than to risk living again. And I truly believed her death was my fault.''

Clayton listened as she spoke, just letting her get it all out. ''I didn't kill Megan. The drunk driver in the other car did that. And as for my parents... well, I won't ever be able to comprehend their sadness or loss. But I know Megan doesn't want me to live in the shadow of her death and I refuse to do it any longer.''

She told him then about finding Megan's journal, about the meeting with her parents. He thanked God and Megan for the miracle they had worked with her and he saw genuine surprise on her face when she told him what her sister had written about her.

''Megan wanted to be more like me,'' she said wondrously. ''And all that time I wished I could be more like her, quiet and studious, selfless and kind.''

"You're more like your sister than you know." He paused, taking a deep breath. "Lucy, how badly were you injured in the accident?"

Lucy shook her head. "I didn't feel physical pain at the time," she said softly. "They gave me medication for that. It was the emotional pain they couldn't take away."

Clayton pinned her with a look that demanded an answer. "Tell me."

Lucy was silent for so long he thought maybe he'd pushed too much, until she spoke. "I had some broken ribs and a dislocated shoulder," she said quietly. "My right leg was broken in two places and I had some internal injuries."

"Good God!" He reached out and took her hands in his, knowing how lucky he was that she had survived that rainy night. Thanking heaven above that she had walked into the Roadhouse and straight into his life. "I'm sorry you had to go through that on top of everything else."

"And I'm sorry I sent you away," she said, surprising him all over again. "I'm sorry I hurt you. I didn't have the courage then or the strength to risk taking a chance in life again. You were something I couldn't control my reaction to and I...guess I panicked."

Clayton couldn't fight a grin. "I don't think I've stirred panic in a woman before."

"You stirred a lot more than that in me...and you know it." He'd stirred her soul to life again, and he'd opened the door to her heart, breaking through every defence she put before him.

"You see, life is for the living," she said, reciting the words to him. "Nothing is certain. Nothing is promised to us and nothing is forever, except what we hold in our hearts today." She paused and smiled. "My sister told me that."

"They're beautiful words," he said, studying her intently.

"I tried not to like you," she confessed. "I tried not to laugh at your jokes or be secretly pleased when I saw you. But I realize now that you are what I want to hold in my heart today and every day," she said, taking a deep breath. "I'm in love with you, Clayton McKinley. I think it started when you came back the night of the fire." She met his gaze with a sure one of her own. "Will you marry me?"

Clayton wondered if he'd imagined her words then decided he wasn't that far gone. Even if he was, he didn't want to recover any time soon. "No."

The stunned expression on Lucy's face didn't begin to match the fear his word had stoked in her eyes. She nodded. "I understand. I treated you cruelly and—"

"Stop talking, Lucy." He stood and pulled her to her feet. "You didn't let me finish."

She scowled. "There's more? I think no pretty much sums it up."

Clayton grinned then because he couldn't help it. He pulled her into his arms and held her to him, their bodies flush with each other, and the minute her body pressed against his, arousal hit him hard and fast. "Oh, there's more, darlin'."

He was quiet for so long, just standing there smiling down at her, that Lucy got impatient. "Well, are you planning to tell me or do I have to guess?"

"I won't marry you," he said obligingly. "Not until I court you."

Lucy's raised eyebrows amused him. "Court me?"

"Yeah, you know, flowers and chocolates, dinner and dancing."

Relief was welcome as it settled around her. She liked playing games with Clayton McKinley, any game he chose, regardless of the rules or the consequences.

"I'm allergic to pollen, chocolates make me fat and dancing isn't something I'll ever be good at."

"There's always horse riding."

Lucy smiled. "Only if we get to ride together."

He kissed her forehead, breathing in the lavender scent he'd missed. "You're a woman after my own heart," he said, grinning like a fool.

"No," she said, her tone sober, her smile fading to something he couldn't pin down, a serenity that was pleasing to watch. "I'm the woman who wants your heart," she said quietly. "And your soul. Your dreams, your children and anything else you want to give me."

Clayton wondered if life got any better than this and then realized it didn't matter. He had what he wanted right here in his arms. "Will you give me those things in return," he asked. "Will you trust me with your heart and soul? With your dreams?"

"Yes," she said, feeling the need to warn him. "McKinley, I'm not an easy person to live with. I'm stubborn and impatient and sometimes I don't stop to think before I act…like that night at the Roadhouse. And the children will always be a part of my life, these ones and the kids that will hopefully follow."

Clayton smiled. "The children are a part of you, part of the love you give to those around you, Lucy. I love you for each of those reasons and so many more we'd grow old right here on this spot if I had to list them all."

Lucy hugged him, wondering how close she'd come to letting him go forever. "That's what I want," she said. "To grow old with you. I guess I'm hoping you're still looking for a miracle...like the one your father found," she said, holding her breath for what seemed like an eternity.

"I found her, all right, stuck by the side of the road one cold night," he replied, his arms tightening around her, his life as close to perfect as he ever expected it to get. "She's clever and funny, she has a beautiful heart that's full of love for anyone who needs it and she makes lousy coffee."

Lucy drew back, her arms still clutching his waist, a frown on her face. "You can make the coffee from now on," she said. "I'll be too busy making babies, keeping Harrison House filled with kids and loving my handsome husband."

"Courting should be an exercise in self-control," he said, smiling at her confused frown. "Our baby making will be done with a ring on your finger."

Lucy smiled. "Is that another McKinley trait?"

"No, it's a tradition," he replied, searching her face for any sign of uncertainty and finding none. "McKinley men only make babies with women they love...and only after they're married. Apart from the fact that my mother would come down and clip me around the ears for doing it any other way, I want to do everything right with you."

"As long as you love me, everything will be fine."

"You're the miracle I've waited my whole life for. I'll always love you, Lucy Warner."

Lucy remembered the one thing they hadn't resolved, one very important thing they'd overlooked.

"Does that mean we'll have no more secrets from each other?"

"None."

Lucy smiled, knowing she had him right where she wanted him. "Then I want to know how you got the lights to go out the night you won the bet."

Clayton was taken completely by surprise and realized he'd been caught. No more secrets meant just that, but instead of asking him some deep question, she wanted to know if he'd cheated. "Faulty wiring, darlin'. Let's put it down to fate and not question it."

Lucy wasn't sure she believed him but maybe the magic would be never quite knowing if he'd done it deliberately.

"I've got other plans," he said, leaning his head toward hers, brushing his lips against hers, tasting the promise of so much more. It was a kiss of homecoming and Lucy didn't hold back, giving herself in a way she never had before, heart and soul, mind and body, to him.

He held her so gently but Lucy didn't want gentle. She wound her arms around his neck, pulling her body closer to his, deepening the kiss until he moaned and then pushing him further.

When it ended they were both battling for breath, but Lucy recovered first. "You won't always find it so easy to distract me, McKinley."

"The name's Clayton," he said with a cocky grin, his eyes so close she could see the deep swirling blue of desire. "And I think we should finish the 'kiss and make up' part."

Lucy laughed at his evasive manoeuvres. "We already made up."

"Even better. We can go straight back to kissing."

"You always have a plan, don't you?"

"I don't need a plan. I have a miracle," he said, his words a promise, a pledge...a gift. "I've got all I'll ever need right here."

He looked at her with such love that Lucy knew her heart was safe with this man. She'd found something that would last beyond forever and she would love him at least that long. He kissed her again, long and hard, then released her reluctantly. "Did the kids know you were coming here?"

Lucy nodded. "They're waiting in the house with your family. Since I told everyone I was coming down here to propose to you, I think we can safely assume the suspense is driving them all mad."

Clayton grinned. "Then let's go put them out of their misery, darlin'."

They walked from the shed arm in arm and Lucy didn't care if she got as dusty and sweaty as he was. Happiness had banished everything else from her mind. She'd survived the accident that night for a reason.

To travel the road she had, the road that had brought her to this place, to this man. Out of all the people in the world and all the roads she could have taken, she'd found Clayton just as she'd been meant to.

The journey Megan had written about was just beginning and Lucy knew she would take her sister's memory with her every step of the way. Megan had reached through time, past death, and she had taught Lucy about courage, about risk and reward. Gray was right, she realized, remembering a long-ago conversation they'd had. *Sometimes life is very simple…it's people who complicate it.*

Cable Creek was where she belonged. The McKinleys were the family she wanted to be a part of. With Clayton by her side, in her heart she would face whatever life dealt her.

The doctors had told her that surviving the accident

made her a medical miracle. Being a miracle was special enough, but now she was McKinley's miracle and that made her the luckiest person in the world.

*   *   *   *   *

SILHOUETTE®
MAKES YOU
A STAR!

*Look in the back pages of
all June Silhouette series books to find an
exciting new contest with fabulous prizes!
Available exclusively through Silhouette.*

Don't miss it!

Silhouette®
Where love comes alive™

*P.S. Watch for details on how you can meet
your favorite Silhouette author.*

Silhouette —

where love comes alive—online...

eHARLEQUIN.com

your romantic
books

- ♥ **Shop online!** Visit Shop eHarlequin and discover a wide selection of new releases and classic favorites at great discounted prices.

- ♥ **Read** our daily and weekly Internet exclusive serials, and participate in our interactive novel in the reading room.

- ♥ **Ever dreamed of being a writer?** Enter your chapter for a chance to become a featured author in our Writing Round Robin novel.

• • • • • •

your romantic
life

- ♥ **Check out** our feature articles on dating, flirting and other important romance topics and get your daily love dose with tips on how to keep the romance alive every day.

• • • • • • •

your
community

- ♥ **Have a Heart-to-Heart** with other members about the latest books and meet your favorite authors.

- ♥ **Discuss** your romantic dilemma in the Tales from the Heart message board.

your romantic
escapes

- ♥ **Learn** what the stars have in store for you with our daily Passionscopes and weekly Erotiscopes.

- ♥ **Get** the latest scoop on your favorite royals in Royal Romance.

SINTA1R

Don't miss the reprisal of
Silhouette Romance's popular miniseries

When King Michael of Edenbourg goes missing,

Royally Wed

The Stanbury Crown

his devoted family and loyal subjects make it their mission to bring him home safely!

Their search begins March 2001 and continues through June 2001.

On sale March 2001: **THE EXPECTANT PRINCESS**
by bestselling author **Stella Bagwell** (SR #1504)

On sale April 2001: **THE BLACKSHEEP PRINCE'S BRIDE**
by rising star **Martha Shields** (SR #1510)

On sale May 2001: **CODE NAME: PRINCE**
by popular author **Valerie Parv** (SR #1516)

On sale June 2001: **AN OFFICER AND A PRINCESS**
by award-winning author **Carla Cassidy** (SR #1522)

Available at your favorite retail outlet.

Silhouette®
Where love comes alive™

Visit Silhouette at www.eHarlequin.com

SRRW3

In July 2001

New York Times bestselling author

DEBBIE MACOMBER

joins

DIANA PALMER

&

Patricia Knoll

in

TAKE5

Volume 1

These five tender love stories
are quick reads, great escapes
and deliver five times the love.

Plus

With $5.00 worth of coupons inside,
this is one sweet deal!

HARLEQUIN®
Makes any time special®

Visit us at www.eHarlequin.com   HNCPV1

SILHOUETTE *Romance*

COMING NEXT MONTH

#1522 AN OFFICER AND A PRINCESS—Carla Cassidy
Royally Wed: The Stanburys

Military law forbade their relationship, but couldn't stop the feelings
Adam Sinclair and Princess Isabel Stanbury secretly harbored. Could
they rescue the king, uncover the conspirators—*and* find the happily-
ever-after they yearned for?

#1523 HER TYCOON BOSS—Karen Rose Smith
25th Book

Mac Nightwalker was wary of gold-digging women, but struggling
single mom Dina Corcoran's money woes touched the cynical tycoon.
He offered her a housekeeping job, and Dina quickly turned Mac's
house into the home he'd never had. Did the brooding bachelor dare let
his Cinderella slip away?

#1524 A CHILD FOR CADE—Patricia Thayer
The Texas Brotherhood

Years earlier, Abby Garson had followed her father's wishes and
married another, although her heart belonged to Cade Randell. Now
Cade was back in Texas. But Abby had been keeping a *big* secret
about the little boy Cade was becoming very attached to....

#1525 THE BABY SEASON—Alice Sharpe
An Older Man

Babies, babies everywhere! A population explosion at Jack Wheeler's
ranch didn't thrill producer Roxanne Salyer—she didn't think she was
mommy material. But Jack's little girl didn't find anything lacking in
Roxanne's charms, and neither did the divorced doctor daddy....

#1526 BLIND-DATE BRIDE—Myrna Mackenzie

Tired of fielding the prospective husbands her matchmaking brothers
tossed her way, Lilah Austin asked Tyler Westlake to be her pretend
beau. Then Tyler realized that he didn't want anyone to claim Lilah
but him! What was a determined bachelor to do...?

#1527 THE LITTLEST WRANGLER—Belinda Barnes

They'd shared a night of passion—and a son James Scott knew
nothing about. Until Kelly Matthews showed up with a toddler—
the spitting image of his daddy! When the time came for Kelly to
return to college, could James convince her he wanted both of them
to stay...forever?

RSCNM0501